Matt Hendrick Telemasses to planet of Avoeli, Fomalhaut IV, in order to track down and rescue his kidnapped daughter. What he finds on the easy going backwater colony is a bizarre religious cult and a race of aliens whose rituals promise to bring the dead back to life. Accompanied by the enigmatic Tiana Tandra, herself attempting to locate a missing loved one, they discover the terrible secret buried deep in the heart of the Avoelian jungle.

FAMADIHANA ON FOMALHAUT IV

THE TELEMASS QUARTET

ERIC BROWN

2014

Jacket art by Tomislav Tikulin.
Book design by Pedro Marques.
Text set in Perpetua.
Titles set in Corporate.

Printed in England by T. J. International.

PS Publishing Ltd
Grosvenor House
1 New Road
Hornsea, HU18 1PG
England
E-mail: editor@pspublishing.co.uk
Visit our website at www.pspublishing.co.uk.

PART ONE

THE
TELEMASS
QUARTET

FAMADIHANA
ON
FOMALHAUT
IV

ONE

ONE SECOND HE WAS STANDING on the translation pad of the Telemass Station at Paris, Earth, and the next he was twenty-five light years away on the planet of Avoeli, Fomalhaut IV.

As ever, the transition was not without its side effects. He felt as if he'd been hit in the chest by an industrial laser, and for a few seconds he wondered where he was. He staggered, as if pushed through a doorway by a particularly forceful hand, then regained his balance. The majority of those around him had managed the transition without batting an eyelid, though one or two were suffering the consequences of being stripped down to the molecular level and fired off on a tachyon vector light years through space.

As his nausea abated, his memory returned. He was on Avoeli, here on a tip-off that he would at last find what he'd been searching for.

The travellers moved off the pad towards the sliding glass door of the reception centre. Medics moved among them, checking for signs of mental and physical distress. A woman approached Hendrick and smiled. "We have a recuperation lounge available, sir, if you would care to follow me."

She led him into a sumptuous bubble that obtruded from the elevated superstructure. This station was built on a tripod of scimitar legs—one of the early models—and it commanded a panoramic view of the surrounding jungle and the capital city embedded in the brilliant greenery.

He sat on a foam-form and accepted a tumbler of nutrient fluid from the woman. "If you don't mind, I'd like to run a few minor diagnostic procedures. These are entirely routine."

"Of course." He was accustomed to being treated like a child every time he took a Telemass journey. His body should have become accustomed to the trauma by now, having endured dozens of translations over the course of his working life, but if anything the side effects were worse with every trip.

The woman ran a handheld scanner over his head and chest, reading the results on a softscreen. She was small and slim, and from the cast of her features and black skin, he guessed she was a descendant of the original Madagascan settlers. They had founded the colony two hundred years ago, when starships had crossed the gulfs of space, before the invention of the Telemass process.

He sipped the nutrient fluid, a sweet, pleasant-tasting fruit juice. Sunlight streamed in through the convex glass walls; the hemisphere of the massive sun was climbing over the far horizon. He'd arrived in the middle of a long Avoeli day, which lasted for some thirty standard hours.

The woman smiled. "You're fine," she said. "No damage done, Mr . . . ?"

"Hendrick. Matt Hendrick."

"Have you come to my world on business, Mr Hendrick?" Her English was stilted, hesitant.

"Pleasure," he lied.

"Then there is much to see here. The jungle is beautiful, and of course the falls are famous throughout the Expansion. Further inland, the Yola Mountain Range is spectacular."

He finished the juice. "The name Avoeli . . . ?"

She smiled as if this were a common question. "My people decided not to follow the Expansion norm and give their planet a Terran name. 'Avoeli' is what the native aliens, the Avoel, call this world. It was considered . . . courteous to adopt their own name for the planet."

Hendrick had had little time to read up on the world before booking his transit here, and he knew next to nothing about the Avoel. It was not unusual for humans to live side by side with native aliens—he'd encountered many such arrangements in his travels—and he was always intrigued by societies that had grown up in such situations. He was intrigued by the interactions—or lack thereof—and by the cultural influences and prejudices that inevitably came about.

"And the Avoel . . . Is there much contact between your peoples?"

Something passed across her features—a quick, tell-tale tightening of the skin about her mouth, as if his question had touched a raw nerve.

She pocketed her scanner and said, "Very little," in a dismissive tone. "There," she went on. "All done. I'd advise you to get a few hours sleep, Mr Hendrick, and then go out this evening to watch the amazing sunset from one of the many restaurants in the city."

"I'll do that," he said, then thanked her and left the lounge.

He passed through a cursory customs check, collected his luggage, then took the elevator down to the street and stepped into the blazing Avoeli noon.

Appallassy was a small city as capitals went, consisting mainly of single-storey timber buildings laid out on a grid pattern of wide streets. The sight was a novelty after coming from Earth, where such a profligate use of timber had been proscribed decades ago. Electric cars beetled along the boulevards, and crowds of brightly dressed colonists promenaded through a market set out on wide sidewalks.

The city perched on the edge of an equatorial plateau, lining the lip of an escarpment overlooking the jungle far below. The predominant shade was green, though of a deeper hue than in the jungles of Earth, and here and there tall purple spikes erupted from the jungle canopy to remind the visitor that this was indeed an alien world.

He'd had no time to pre-book accommodation, but a terrace of small hotels lined the escarpment along from the Telemass Station. He was tired—it had been late evening in Paris when he'd departed—and he thought it wise to take the medic's recommendation and rest. Later, when he'd slept, he'd start his investigations by enquiring at the hotels in the vicinity.

He booked into an establishment calling itself the Malagasy Retreat, saying he'd stay for two nights, maybe more, and was shown to a quiet room overlooking a terraced garden that tumbled down the escarpment.

He sat on the bed, brought up a series of pictures on his wrist-com, and stared at them until the succession of images became too painful to bear. Then he switched off his com, lay down, and was soon fast asleep.

———

If Lalla were here, she'd tell me if I'd done the right thing.

As soon as the tall, blonde woman appeared on the translation pad, I was drawn to her. I don't normally go for forty-year-old whites, but this woman had elegance and poise. Also, she was showing the effects of translation nausea.

We got talking. She was with a man, but he hung back. We arranged to meet in a bar later, and I wondered where this might lead. She didn't look bi, but you can never tell.

So we met, had a drink. Her name is Maatje, and she's from the Netherlands, Earth. She didn't say what she was doing here, but she did say that she was being followed.

Then I found out what she wanted from me, and I felt disappointed. I thought she might have been interested in me, not what I might be able to do for her.

Anyway, I agreed.

Call me weak . . . but she is beautiful.

Lalla would hate me . . . but she did run off like that, so . . .

Christ, Lalla, where are you?

—

The sunset was indeed amazing.

He selected the Faro Bar, a short stroll along from his hotel, because that was where many Terran tourists had chosen to watch the sun go down. They sat at tables on the wide, stepped terraces, drank local cocktails, and gasped at the view.

For the past two hours, since awaking from a dreamless sleep, he'd moved from hotel to hotel along the boulevard. With the inducement of the local currency he'd persuaded staff to speak with him briefly and to examine the series of pix he carried on his wrist-com. He covered more than twenty hotels, but to no avail. The people he was seeking were not staying at any of the establishments he ventured into.

He ordered a beer and stood by the rail of the terrace, listening to nearby conversations and watching the bloated hemisphere of the sun slip slowly over the horizon. Though Avoeli was the seventh planet from its primary, it was still close enough so that great loops and spumes of molten ejecta could be seen spouting from the sun as it sank.

"In the week we've been here," a woman said in French to her male companion, "this is the most spectacular . . ."

Hendrick moved on. The people he was attempting to locate had come to Avoeli—or so his sources had told him—three days ago.

He stood beside a knot of Europeans—a business delegation from Germany, he gathered from their conversation. They sipped at small glasses of local beer as if it were poison and talked about a convention in the morning. He glanced among them and recognised a woman he'd seen on the translation pad that day. So, they had arrived at the same time as he had. He moved on.

He stepped down the terrace, listening into the conversation of obvious tourists and ignoring the knots of locals. He heard a dozen languages—European, Asian, and a couple he didn't recognise but guessed were a local patois—and settled next to a group of holiday-makers speaking loud Spanish and knocking back Avoeli beer with relish.

He smiled at a tall, elegant middle-aged woman in a flower-patterned dress and made some non sequitur about the sunset. "I've only just arrived, so I'm still in awe."

She laughed a little drunkenly. "Well so am I, and I came in on the Paris transmission three days ago."

His heart kicked. "But what a coincidence. Friends of mine were on that very transmission. I had arranged to meet them here today, but . . . "

She laid a tipsy hand on his arm and laughed. "Well, I think you should join our party and celebrate the sunset, no?"

He smiled. "Why not? But perhaps you've seen my friends . . . ?" And he activated his com and brought up the pix.

The woman squinted at the images, began to shake her head, and then caught herself. "One moment. Carlos, Carlos! Isn't this the woman you were charming before her husband returned?"

A long-haired young man looked at Hendrick and glanced at the picture on the screen. He nodded, muttering something in Catalan about an ice maiden.

"A friend of mine," Hendrick said.

The woman interrupted, "Carlos, the gentleman here is trying to locate the lady and her husband."

The young man shrugged. "She said they were taking the train into the interior. That would be yesterday."

"Did she say where they were heading?"

Carlos frowned and shook his head. "Didn't say, or I don't remember. Sorry. She just said the interior."

"Well, thanks anyway." Hendrick called the waiter for another round of beers.

The evening wore on, and he extricated himself from the attention of the Spanish woman and moved along the terrace. He wished to be alone with his thoughts.

The night was warm and scented with an alien perfume from flowers the size of dinner plates. He sat at a table and lodged his feet on the rail, staring down at the darkening jungle and the last filaments and flares of the sun as it vanished over the edge of the world. If he were not here on business, he told himself, he might have been able to enjoy the pleasures of the city and the surrounding jungle.

At first light tomorrow he would make his way to the monorail station and attempt to find out where his 'friends' might have travelled to yesterday. It was a lead, though a slight one. He told himself that he should be content with this, so early in his investigations.

His attention was attracted by a group of people along the terrace to his right. They were locals, talking animatedly in the sing-song Malagasy tongue. Some wore the red uniforms of the Telemass Organisation, but the medic who'd administered to his needs that morning was out of uniform. She wore a short, tight-fitting yellow dress which contrasted startlingly with her chestnut skin. He had not noticed her hair that morning—it had been swept back and concealed by a beret—but now it trailed in a comet's tail of dreadlocks intertwined with multi-coloured ribbons.

She appeared a little drunk, swaying as she spoke to a tall, older woman in a Telemass uniform. The woman appeared uninterested in what the younger woman was saying, and she allowed her attention to wander.

The medic sighed and looked away; her eyes met Hendrick's and, after a second of confusion, smiled in recognition. Hendrick looked away, not wanting her drunken attention.

Seconds later, she left the group and swayed across to him. She lodged herself precariously on the edge of a chair and pressed a long-nailed forefinger to his chest.

"Now . . . I know you! Don't tell me. I never . . . never forget a name! No, don't tell me."

He drained his beer and was about to stand up, on the pretext of going to the bar, when she said, "Hendrick, that's it! Matt Hendrick!"

He smiled, despite his annoyance. "Well done," he said. "Now, if you don't mind . . . "

"What?" She opened her eyes wide. "You're going? But we've hardly said hello!"

"I'm sorry. I really must . . ."

"What? You're going to take the train to the interior, looking for . . . for whoever it is you're looking for?"

He stared at her. "How do you know?"

"I'm a telepath," she said. She attempted to keep a straight face, but the alcohol in her system would not comply. "Not really. I overheard you speaking earlier with the tourists, silly! I was just behind you."

"Ah . . ."

He activated his wrist-com and showed her the pix. "You might have seen her, spoken to her . . . She was with a tall, good-looking man."

She squinted at the pix and nodded. "I saw her. I mean, how could I miss her. She's beautiful . . ."

"But you didn't speak?"

She shook her head. "No. She . . . She wasn't suffering the after-effects of the transmission like you."

He nodded and made to get up.

Her huge eyes registered pantomime disappointment. "You're going so soon?"

"I have a train to catch."

She pressed her finger against his chest again. "You won't catch a train at this time of night, my friend."

"I won't? And why is that?"

"Because the Avoel won't allow it."

He stared at her. "They won't?"

She put the neck of her beer bottle to her full lips, tilted the bottle, and drank. "It's because . . . because they don't like people travelling at night. The darkness is sacred. As is the sky. That . . . That's why they don't

7

allow air-cars either. Just ground cars and monotrains. The sky is sacred, not to be violated. And . . . And as we are guests on their planet, we must comply. So the founding fathers and mothers of our colony agreed, two hundred years ago."

Something in her tone prompted him to ask, "And what do you think of the Avoel?"

She stared at him, blinking. "I . . . I think they are evil," she said, surprising him.

"You do? And why is that?"

Her face crumpled and she wept. She made an instant effort at recovery, wiping her wet cheeks with the inside of her wrists and saying, "It's nothing! Ignore me. I'm drunk."

She looked up, attracted the attention of a waiter, and ordered two more beers.

When they came, she took a small sip and smiled at Hendrick. "So . . . will you tell me why you are looking for . . . for these people?"

"It's a private matter. I can't discuss it."

She pulled a prim frown, mocking him. "Are you a detective? Is that it? Do you detect missing people?"

"No, nothing like that," he said, wondering if she were indeed a telepath. "But . . . tell me, if the people I need to trace left on a train yesterday, bound for the interior, have you any idea where they might have been heading?"

She sat suddenly upright on her chair, staring at him. "On Thursdays . . . there is only one train, and it stops only at its destination, Allay."

"So they must have alighted there?"

She nodded, hiccupped, and took another swallow of beer.

"And is there a train to Allay tomorrow?"

She nodded. "At two."

He saluted her with his beer. "Thank you . . . " he began.

"Tiana," she said, supplying her name with a smile. "Tiana Tandra."

He made to rise and said, "My thanks, Tiana. Perhaps we'll meet again when I leave Avoeli."

He could see her come to some decision, and a split-second later she jumped from her chair into his lap. He was surprised by her lightness, and

8

then by his involuntary reaction to the pressure of her bottom against his groin. She moved her lips to his ear and whispered, "Take me back to your hotel, Mr Hendrick. Matt."

He felt the warmth of her flesh through her dress. How long had it been since his wife had left him, since he'd last felt a woman like this? He'd avoided such contact, telling himself that it would only remind him of Maatje's betrayal.

He said, "I never take advantage, Tiana, of drunken women," and felt like a prude.

"In that case . . . " She looked over his shoulder and snapped something in her own language to a passing waiter. He stopped, reached into his pocket, and produced a silver blister-pack. She passed the man a crumpled banknote, pressed out a pill, and held it up before Hendrick's eyes.

"Sobertab," she said, placing it on her tongue. She took a mouthful of beer, swallowed, and stared at him.

"There, now I am as sober a . . . a, what do you say, a magistrate?"

Smiling, he eased her from his lap and stood up. "And, sober, you realise that you've just propositioned a total stranger and . . . "

"Not so fast, Matt." She laid a hand on his chest tenderly. "Look, I'm taking the same train as you tomorrow. I . . . There's something I must do in the jungle town where the train stops. So . . . we can accompany each other." She smiled. "I'll be your guide. And I . . . I might even be able to help you find who you're looking for."

He stared at her, wondering where this might lead.

She said, "So . . . I'm sober now, Matt Hendrick. Will you *please* take me back to your hotel?"

TWO

HE WAS AWOKEN IN THE EARLY HOURS by the sound of her quiet sobbing. She lay beside him on her stomach, the moonlight delineating the undulating curve of her back. She pressed her face into the pillow as if not wanting to wake him with her crying.

He rolled from the bed, crossed to the window, and pulled open the curtain. Ivory light cascaded into the room, and he stared out in surprise at the beauty of the double moons sailing high above the darkened jungle.

He returned and sat beside her on the bed. She turned quickly and stared up at him.

"Tell me," he said, thumbing tears from her cheeks.

She turned over and shuffled herself up against the headboard, drawing her knees up to her small breasts. She didn't meet his gaze as she said, "I'm sorry. I didn't mean to wake you. It's nothing."

"Nothing is making you cry like this? And nothing made you sob last night, when you were still drunk? I'd hate to see you when you're really upset."

She spluttered a laugh. "I mean . . . It's nothing I want to trouble you with."

He almost shrugged, said okay, and returned to bed. But something about the woman—the way she had made love to him earlier with a tenderness and urgency that belied the idea that he was a mere casual pickup—made him want to help her.

"Tell me, Tiana," he said, "and I'll tell you why I'm really here."

She stared at him, her big eyes glistening in the moonlight. He took in her nakedness. He found it hard to tell how old she was. Her skin was flawless, tight like an athlete's over well-developed muscles. She might

10

have been anything from twenty to thirty-five.

She murmured, "Last night I said I had business to do in Allay . . . "

"That's right. I recall. But what business?"

"It's hard to explain."

He said, "You're looking for someone, right?"

He was gratified by her surprised reaction. "That's right. But how . . . ?"

It was merely an intuition, based on experience: her drunkenness last night, her sexual recklessness in propositioning him, her heartfelt tears. A lover had left her, and Tiana was at a loss to work out what to do.

"A lucky guess," he said. "Tell me."

She shrugged. "I love her. We've been together for three years now. She . . . Her mother is part of the Church, but Lalla told me she wanted nothing to do with it."

"The Church?" His interest quickened. His contact back on Earth had told him that Maatje was interested in some colonial religious cult here on Avoeli. Could this cult have something to do with the Church, he wondered?

"They . . . they don't exactly worship the Avoel gods, or perhaps they do. They're very secretive. Outsiders aren't allowed in, except after months of vetting.

"And Lalla?"

"Her mother wanted her to be . . . It's like christening, a ceremony that happens in every disciple's twenty-fifth year. Lalla was . . . drawn to the belief system."

"You told me that she wanted nothing to do with the Church?"

She looked up at him. "That's what she told me, Matt, but I'm not sure I believe her. She . . . "Tiana shrugged. "She had a very complex relationship with the Church. I suppose it's inevitable, if you're brought up to believe nothing else but what everyone around you says is the truth."

"What do they believe?"

She shrugged her slim shoulders again. "The Avoel have many gods. It's a form of animism. Nature worship."

He opened his mouth in a silent "Ah . . . "

He said, "When you told me, last night, that you thought the aliens were evil . . . "

She rubbed tears from her eyes with the heels of her thumbs, then shook her head. "That was the drink talking. I don't think they're evil, just . . . incomprehensible." She smiled like a little girl caught out. "We sometimes think the worst of what we can't understand, don't we?"

"You're right," he said. "Tell me what happened."

"We had a row. I wanted Lalla to have nothing to do with the Church. They . . . The congregation, I find them creepy. They believe in nothing I believe in. They thought my relationship with Lalla . . . Well, they're against it. They're against all forms of what they call . . . promiscuity."

"And you, of course, are not?"

"Isn't it normal to want to express affection and at the same time take pleasure in your desires?"

"I would say so, yes. But the Expansion is a big place, and in some places that would be seen as immoral, even evil."

He smiled at the contradiction within him, for while he agreed with Tiana, he found it hard to live by that code. He was the product of parents who were of strict Dutch Calvinist stock, and what was inculcated from an early age died hard. Which was probably why when he found and married Maatje he had felt so fulfilled . . . and why her leaving him had hurt so much.

He had surprised himself last night when he'd turned his back on his inhibitions and enjoyed making love to Tiana; it had been a release, a catharsis after so long.

"And after the argument?" he asked.

She gestured with a forlorn hand. "She just . . . went."

"And do you know where?"

She pulled a face. "I thought perhaps Allay."

"And what is at Allay?"

She regarded her small fingers, intertwined on the summit of her knees. "The aliens, the Avoel . . . It is a holy place for them." She looked up at him. "But I honestly don't know if she has gone there, or if so why."

He thought about it. "Did you live together?"

She looked surprised. "Why do you ask?"

"I'd like to examine her belongings. See if there might be some clue as to where she went and why."

12

Tiana shook her head. "She has an apartment in town. I have a pin-key, though."

"Perhaps we should take a look."

She nodded and was silent for a time. At last she said, "Why are you helping me like this?"

"When you asked me last night if I looked for missing people . . . Well, I did once. I worked for the European Police Agency in Amsterdam, in the missing persons department."

"Do you think we'll be able to find Lalla?"

"We'll do our best, okay?"

It was a lead, and the best he'd had for months. Was it too much to hope that at last he was on the verge of finding Maatje and his daughter?

"Matt, you said you'd tell me what you were really doing here."

He reached out and pressed his finger to her lips. "Not now."

He lay down beside Tiana, stared up at the ceiling, and tried to sleep.

When he awoke a little later, Tiana was no longer in bed. She was curled in the window seat, murmuring something into her wrist-com.

———

Why do I always feel so damned guilty? All my life, every minute of it, I'm hounded by guilt.

I remember when I was little, my mother had this ability to just look at me and make me feel as if I'd done something wrong. And later, when I was thirteen, me and Lalla . . . The pleasure made the guilt all the more intense. And when my mother found out . . .

And Lalla makes me feel guilty all the time. I've tried to explain that I love her, that she's the only person I'll ever truly love. And she says, So why can't you be faithful, and I say, But I am faithful, in my heart, where it matters. But she doesn't understand, and I can't explain.

And now this.

Maatje told me he was cruel and vindictive—a bastard, she'd said.

The thing is, I can't see that. He's quiet and kind and thoughtful. A little sad. It's strange how people's perceptions of the same person can be so very different.

I like Matt Hendrick a lot, which is why what I've done makes me feel so guilty.

13

They walked through the quiet town just after dawn. A tropical rain had rinsed the land and laced the streets with a billion scintillating sequins. The air was warm but fresh, the scent of alien blooms accentuated by the downpour.

After the overcrowded cities of Europe, Appallassy was like paradise.

As he walked beside the silent Tiana, Hendrick reflected that one day he would like to make his home on a colony world; somewhere sparsely populated and rural, away from industry and commerce and crowds. He was in his mid-thirties and hankered after a tranquil life.

Perhaps one day, when he'd found what he was looking for.

"You live on a beautiful world."

"You don't really see what you see every day, do you?" she said. "I mean, it's hard to appreciate anything when you have nothing to judge it against."

"You've never left Avoeli?"

"No. Isn't that strange? I work for the Telemass Organisation, and yet I've never set foot on another world."

"Why not?"

"It's expensive, for starters, even though as an employee of the organisation I'd get discounted fares."

"Would you like to travel?"

"Of course! I've seen holo-docs, read about other worlds in the Expansion." She glanced at him. "Have you travelled a lot?"

"In my twenties part of my job was to liaise with police forces around the Expansion. I suppose I've visited more than fifty colony worlds."

"Fifty!" She laughed. "I can't imagine . . . That must have been amazing."

"I suppose it was, in the early days. It's surprising what you get used to, though. Towards the end . . . Well, it became just another job."

"But you said that you no longer looked for missing people . . . And yet you're here, looking for someone?"

"I retired from the force a couple of years ago," he said, and left it at that.

They were walking down a quiet residential street lined with timber houses, each one surrounded by tropical trees and shrubs.

"So," Tiana said, "what do you do now?"

He told her the truth. "Very little. I inherited some money when my father died. That's when I quit the force."

"So, you lead a life of leisure?"

"You could say that."

"And you live on Earth?"

"Near Amsterdam, Europe. But . . . one day I'd like to settle down on a colony world."

She laughed. "And I'd like nothing more than to travel to all the big, busy planets of the Expansion."

"You're a medic, no? You could easily travel, find work."

"I have a general nursing qualification, so I suppose I could work anywhere."

"What's kept you here, apart from the prohibitive cost of Telemass travel?"

"What's kept me here? Lalla, I suppose." She glanced at him. "Are you married, Matt?"

He stared ahead. "Was."

"It's amazing what you do for love, isn't it? Or rather, what you don't do for love, in my case."

"Yes," he said, "it is." He looked at her, at her big eyes and flawless skin. "How old are you?"

"Twenty-four," she replied. "What? You look surprised."

"You're wise beyond your years." He hoped he didn't sound patronising.

Smiling, she stopped in the street and pointed. "Here we are."

She led him through the overgrown garden of a single-storey weatherboard house, inserted a pin in the front door and gestured him in before her.

The door opened straight into a lounge hung with tapestries and prints showing local jungle scenes. The furnishings were old and battered, and the room had a cosy, bohemian feel.

He stood in the centre of the room and turned.

"What are you looking for?"

"I don't know, but I will when I find it. When did you last see Lalla?"

"Four days ago. I stayed here the night. We were due to meet for coffee in town the following day. She never turned up."

"And that's not like her?"

15

"She always keeps her appointments. Or if she can't make it, she contacts me."

"And you've tried contacting her?"

She raised her arm, indicating her wrist-com. "All the time, constantly since then."

"And nothing?"

"Only a message saying that a connection was unavailable."

"And she's never gone off like this before. After a row, perhaps?"

"Never."

Pinned to the wall above a desk was a series of pix depicting slim, pale humanoids with big eyes, no visible noses, and wide mouths bearing prominent, shark-like teeth. He moved closer and examined the images. The aliens' teeth were at odds with the rest of their appearance. He was put in mind of carnivorous lemurs.

"The Avoel," she said.

"Why does Lalla have these?"

"She's a biologist. She studies them. She's fascinated by the creatures."

"They look . . . odd."

"That's what everyone says when they see them for the first time. It's the teeth."

He nodded. "What are relations like between the colonists and the Avoel?"

"There's very little interaction. The Avoel are jungle dwelling. They're a peaceful race. There's no trouble between us."

"Last night, when you were drunk . . . you said they were evil. I know, I know . . . You said that that was the drink speaking. But there's no smoke without fire . . . " He watched her.

She shrugged, looked away.

"Tiana?"

"Like I said . . . "

"You resent the Avoel because of the hold they have over Lalla, right?"

She bit her lip, staring down at the threadbare rug. She said at last, "I don't like where Lalla's research was leading her."

"Which was where?"

She hesitated then said, "Follow me."

16

Intrigued, he followed her into an adjacent bedroom. A mattress occupied the floor, piled with a mess of bed sheets. The walls were covered with pix showing crowds of colonists bearing what Hendrick took to be stretchers above their heads.

He looked around the room. "What did you want to show me?"

"Have you heard of famadihana?"

"A sex act that would shock my prudish Terran sensibilities?"

She laughed. "It's an old Madagascan tradition. A burial ritual—or, strictly speaking, a *re*-burial ritual."

Ah, the pix on the walls.

"I once read something about it. Remind me."

"My people, centuries ago on Earth, performed what could be translated as 'turning the bones'. Every seven years they exhumed the remains of ancestors and paraded with them around our villages." She gestured to the pictures on the walls. "That's what they are. These images are a couple of centuries old."

He could have mistaken them for pictures of contemporary colonists, so little had the colourful clothing changed over the decades.

Tiana went on. "It was a form of ancestor worship, a way of respecting our dead. The practice died out towards the end of the twenty-first century."

"But what has this to do with Lalla's research?"

Tiana pursed her lips in contemplation. "A few months ago, she made a discovery—something the Church didn't like and wanted kept quiet."

"Go on."

"She was on a field trip in the interior. She's attached to the university here at Appallassy. What she discovered was that . . . " She fell silent, turned from Hendrick, and stared through the window, out at the dense jungle that began metres from the rickety garden fence.

"Tiana?"

"I'm sorry," she said, still with her back to him. "You see, she was threatened that if ever she spoke of what she saw . . . But she told me."

She turned to him, her expression on the verge of desperation. "Now do you understand why I'm so frightened, why I fear she might have been . . . ?"

He reached out and drew her to him, lodged her head against his chest and said, "Tell me."

17

She looked up at him. "When she was in the interior, observing a clan of Avoel, she found that they practised a form of famadihana. She didn't go into detail but said that there was a marked similarity to the old Madagascan ritual."

"But surely a coincidence?"

"She thought so, yes. But even so, she thought her discovery might lead her to getting a research grant."

"And you said someone threatened Lalla to keep quiet about it?"

"That's right. A pastor in the Church."

"What did he say?"

Tiana waved her hand. "That if she publicised her findings, he had friends in high places who would ensure she was expelled from the university. And, well, that if she persisted, then she might expect more . . . physical treatment."

"Why would the Church want to keep the alien practice quiet?"

She stared up at him. "Exactly, Matt. That's what's so troubling."

He crossed to the window and stared out, then turned to her. "The Church here no longer practises famadihana, does it?"

She shook her head, her white teeth nipping her bottom lip. "No. Not to my knowledge."

"Who issued this threat? The pastor's name . . . ?"

She stared at him, her eyes wide. "Father Jacobius."

He stared into the jungle, considering what she'd told him. He glanced at his wrist-com. It was not yet ten, and the monotrain to Allay wasn't due to leave Appallassy until two that afternoon.

"I'd like to pay this Father Jacobius a visit."

Her eyes widened with alarm. "I'm not sure you should."

"Don't worry. I'll make up some story to cover my questions. I just want to find out what's behind this Church and their threats."

"Do you think it might help to find out what happened to Lalla?"

"Well, that's what I hope anyway. It can't do any harm."

She told him where the Church was situated, half a kilometre away, and gave him directions. "I'd better not be seen with you near the place."

He gave Tiana his wrist-com code and they arranged to meet at a café in the centre of town at midday.

THREE

HENDRICK HAD NEVER LOOKED upon a church building without a feeling of revulsion, and he experienced this again as he gazed at the spruce, white-painted weatherboard façade of the Church of the Ultimate Redemption.

He'd once tried to tell his mother what he thought of her Christianity: "It doesn't make sense. Your God is supposedly all-powerful, knows everything, and lives outside time and space. He is one and indivisible—the Father, the Son, the Holy Ghost—and yet, in full knowledge of the consequences, he sent his son to Earth to be crucified and resurrected so that humanity might be forgiven their sins, and this was called a *sacrifice*? But what was sacrificed by this tripartite, omnipotent being, Mother?"

To which she had merely replied, "You don't understand, Matthias. It is all about faith."

And he had given up attempting to talk to her about her belief, and had never looked upon a church—any church—in quite the same way again.

He wondered what corrupted form of belief this particular Church might practise—and if indeed Maatje had been drawn to this cult.

He walked up the pathway to an open timber door and passed over the threshold from bright sunlight to cool shadow. When his eyes adjusted to the gloom, he made out an interior much like every other church the Expansion over, with a central aisle and pews to either side. At the far end was the altar, and on the wall above it a vast timber cross, though the horizontal bar was lower than on the crucifixes of Earth.

The church was deserted. He moved down the aisle and passed through a small door to the right of the altar. This room was empty too. He made out a half-open door that led outside, crossed to it, and stepped out into

19

the sunlight. He found himself in a well-ordered vegetable garden that backed onto the jungle.

A tall, elderly European man in a grey habit was tending a vine at the far end of the garden. He turned and shielded his eyes from the sun as Hendrick emerged.

"I'm sorry to interrupt you," Hendrick said. "I'm looking for Father Jacobius."

The man smiled. He was thin and ascetic-looking, with a hatchet face and piercing grey eyes. His skin was tanned, his cropped hair silver.

"And you have found him," Jacobius said, advancing and taking his hand in a firm shake. "How might I be of assistance?"

Hendrick was surprised; he had expected Jacobius to be an Avoelian of Madagascan descent. He had also expected the pastor to be stern, suspicious—not this overtly friendly, easy-going, smiling man. So much for his prejudices.

He introduced himself, giving a fictitious name and stating that he was a xeno-biologist from the Sorbonne, Earth. "My current studies involve alien cultures and their interaction with human societies," he finished.

"Ah, then you have come to the right place," Jacobius laughed. "Come, would you care for a drink?"

"I'm not keeping you from your work?"

"To be honest, I was rather hoping for a distraction." Jacobius led the way to a shed across the garden, indicated a bench, and disappeared into the shed. He emerged a minute later with two bottles of ice-cold beer.

"I always think that one's labour should be rewarded, Dr Hennessy," he said.

Hendrick drank and asked Jacobius about the Avoel. "I understand the natives of this world are hunter-gatherers with their own animist belief system. I hope to do a little field-work in the jungle north of here."

"You have obtained the requisite permits, I take it?"

Hendrick temporised. "The matter is in hand."

"As far as I know, no academic has come to Avoeli to study the aliens," Jacobius said. "The original exploration team categorised them as pre-industrial sentients and left it at that, which of course meant that our colonisation of the planet met with certain restrictions. We are not allowed to develop the jungle any further than the present limits, for instance, and must respect the Avoel's boundaries, customs, and beliefs."

"Ah, their beliefs . . . "

"They are animists, as you say, Dr Hennessy. They believe that every living thing possesses, for want of a better word, a soul—a spiritual life force, be that insect, animal, or man. It's a very rudimentary belief system that has its analogue in many so-called primitive societies on Earth."

Hendrick sipped his beer. "I heard before I came here that your church's beliefs and the Avoel's share a certain common ground."

Jacobius's hatchet face split in a wide smile. "I think that is stating the case rather too forcefully."

Hendrick glanced at Jacobius for any sign of suspicion, maybe irritation, but only saw the man's ready, good-humoured smile.

"What does your church believe?"

"We are pantheists. We believe that there is more than one divine being that holds sway over this physical realm. While the Avoel believe that each living being is equal—hence their animism—we, on the other hand, believe that our gods created a . . . a hierarchy, if you like."

Hendrick tried to hide his smile. "With humankind at the top?"

"With humankind and all other sentient beings at the summit of this hierarchy, yes. We are there by divine legislature, as it were, but with this elevated position comes a grave responsibility to all creatures in our gods' universe."

Hendrick nodded "I see. So . . . you would say that we and the Avoel are equal?"

"Indubitably."

He took another mouthful of beer, considering his next question. "And does the Church of the Ultimate Redemption worship its ancestors, Father?" He stared at the man, gauging his reaction.

Did he see a hesitation, a shadow cross the holy man's eyes? "The Church's regard for those who have gone before is complex, Doctor. We hold that while our ancestors are dead on a physical plain, their spirits live on in the . . . in the weft and weave, if you like, of the universe. This is beyond time and space, so is, as it were, congruent with our reality and time. While we do not actively worship those that have gone before, we hold them in reverence."

Hendrick nodded, as if comprehending the man's belief system. "And I take that as regards an afterlife . . . ?"

Jacobius smiled. "The afterlife is the weft and weave, which we call the Hallalla."

"And to attain this plain?"

Jacobius smiled. "Everyone attains Hallalla, Doctor."

Hendrick frowned. "Then, I don't quite see . . . What inducement is there, in your belief system, to follow the right way, to lead a virtuous life? If we *all* attain Hallalla, then we might as well all lead hedonistic, vice-laden lives."

"And that is the beauty, the surpassing beauty of our church, my friend; it is one of the reasons why the Church of the Ultimate Redemption is right, while all the other religions of the Expansion are mere figments . . . There is *no* inducement to lead morally just lives—the choice is ours. We choose to follow the ways of the Church and worship the sanctity of all life. In this," he went on, "our creed is analogous to Humanism. Followers of that philosophy too believe that there is no spiritual inducement to lead a just life: they do so for the joy of experiencing the simple, unalloyed miracle of existence in the here and now."

Hendrick stared across at the orderly rows of vegetables, wondering if in Father Jacobius's philosophy he had come across a belief system a little more palatable than the carrot-and-stick inducement of Christianity and similar cults.

He drank his beer, and talk turned to other matters. Jacobius asked him about his work, and Hendrick made up some story about field-work on Chalcedony and his study of the native Ashentay there.

Perhaps an hour later, as he was about to take his leave, a thought occurred to him. "While I'm here, I hope to compare notes with a fellow xeno-biologist," he said, "a student named Lalla Vaugines."

He watched Jacobius for any adverse reaction, but none came. He went on. "I understand she's a member of your church?"

Jacobius smiled. "Not Lalla, but her mother is a valued members of my congregation, yes."

"Lalla is doing some interesting work with the Avoel," Hendrick said, "and I'm looking forward to working with her."

But Jacobius merely smiled and inclined his head politely.

Hendrick hesitated then asked, "I don't suppose a friend of mine from Earth, Maatje Vanderbilt, has contacted you or anyone in your church? She's a fellow academic with an interest in colonial religions, and I thought she'd be on Avoeli . . . but we seem to have missed each other."

There was no reaction on Jacobius's tanned face, not a flicker of recognition in his bright blue eyes. "I'm afraid not, Dr Hennessy."

Hendrick drained his beer. "I've taken up enough of your time, Father Jacobius. You've been most kind. I'll let you get back to work."

"Not at all. I have enjoyed our conversation, and please feel free to drop by at any time."

He showed Hendrick through the church and said farewell on the steps. They shook hands, and Hendrick retraced his steps to the centre of town.

—

I really want to tell him that I met Maatje, tell him what I agreed to do for her. But I can't bring myself to do that: I fear his reaction, his anger. But most of all, I fear that he'll hate me for what I did. The guilt is almost unbearable.

I've never felt this way about a man before. I wonder if it's because . . . No, that's rubbish! Dad walked out when I was five, and I hardly remember him, so I refuse to admit that I'm looking for a substitute figure.

And now Matt has agreed to try to help me find Lalla!

If only I could bring myself to be honest with him.

FOUR

THEY SAT ON THE PATIO OF A CAFÉ on the escarpment overlooking the jungle.

"Father Jacobius seemed entirely reasonable," he told Tiana. "And I've come across worse belief systems."

She looked at him over the process of blowing her coffee. "He didn't give anything away about Lalla?"

Hendrick shook his head. "I mentioned Lalla and that I was in professional contact with her."

"How did he react?"

"I didn't detect anything untoward in his manner. As I said, he seemed reasonable, very friendly." He hesitated. "He didn't seem like the kind of man who would issue threats. Which doesn't mean that he didn't."

"Did you ask him about the Avoel?"

"He told me about their belief system, and he distanced his church's beliefs from theirs. He was, as the saying goes, playing his cards close to his chest."

"What I'd like to know is why the Church doesn't want Lalla, or anyone else, investigating the Avoel."

"He said that no academics had ever studied the aliens, to the best of his knowledge."

"And he wants to keep it that way." She shrugged. "Perhaps we'll find out more when we get to Allay."

"I said that I hoped to do some field-work, and Jacobius mentioned that I'd need a permit."

"If we were to enter the jungle around Allay, yes." She waved this away. "But no one ever checks."

He considered the journey ahead and the aliens. "We could meet with the Avoel? They wouldn't be hostile?"

She smiled. "Hostile? The Avoel? Despite their teeth, they're gentle, passive."

"Could we communicate with them?"

"Some of them do speak a little Malagasy, yes."

"Have you ever met one?"

"Never. They keep themselves to themselves. They come nowhere near the town, but I've glimpsed them from the train from time to time in the jungle. They're small, quick creatures."

"And you think Lalla has gone to Allay?"

She stared at her coffee and murmured, "If the Church hasn't carried out its threat of violence."

He contrasted that idea with the peaceable Father Jacobius; the two didn't sit side by side that easily.

Tiana smiled at him. "But when we get to Allay, Matt, we might find her working away as if nothing has happened."

"I hope so. Do you know where she worked?"

"She was interested in an old Avoel temple in the jungle to the north of the town. We could start there."

He sipped his coffee—dark and rich and, according to Tiana, grown locally on the terraces that stepped down to the jungle below. He watched the locals on the patio: the men in shorts and bright shirts, the women in flowing gowns and turban-like headgear. The predominant colours were red, green, and white, which matched the planetary flag of Avoeli and that of the old Malagasy nation.

Tiana's wrist-com chimed. Hendrick watched her as she took the call.

"Yes . . . Yes, I do. Of course." Her eyes widened. "That's an odd coincidence. Lalla is too. No, I don't."

She listened to what the caller was saying, her face pulled into a frown.

"I could, yes. I'm not leaving until two. I have someone with me, a . . . a detective from Earth. Would it be okay if he came along?" She nodded. "Good. We'll be there in five minutes."

She cut the connection and looked up at him. "Very strange. That was an old colleague of Lalla's mother, a retired professor from the university."

"What did she want?"

Tiana shrugged. "Lalla's mother is missing and she's concerned. She's tried contacting Lalla but couldn't reach her."

"Where does she live?"

Tiana pointed along the escarpment. "Not far from the station. We could drop by before we take the train."

"I'll just settle the bill and then we'll get off."

At the bar, he looked back at Tiana, her bare feet drawn up on her chair, murmuring into her wrist-com. She looked incredibly beautiful.

———

That thing about people's differing perceptions again . . .

Lalla never had a good word to say about Father Jacobius. She said he was an evil, scheming, manipulative charlatan who was using the credulity of the faithful to line his own pockets. She went on about all his shady business dealings, and I must admit that they sounded corrupt. According to Lalla, he had the police and the politicians in his pocket, paying huge bribes out of church funds.

And yet Matt says he appeared entirely reasonable . . .

And now this. Lalla's mother has gone missing too.

———

The exclusive residences of Appallassy, according to Tiana, were owned by rich business-people and staff of the university—sprawling, multilevel villas that clung to the incline of the escarpment with spectacular views over the lower plain.

"What do you know about this woman?" Hendrick asked as they paused on the zigzag path that led to the entrance of the professor's villa.

The red tiles of the villa showed through a canopy of trees. Tropical birds called deafeningly and clattered through the branches. "Not a lot. She was an anthropologist who taught Lalla. She's a close friend of Lalla's mother."

"A member of the Church?"

"Not that I'm aware, no."

She led the way down the winding path and pushed open a swing gate. They batted their way through a riotous garden, which was almost indistinguishable from the jungle that began in earnest a little further down the incline, and came at last to a smart weatherboard villa.

A handsome woman in her sixties with a thin face and short, iron-grey hair sat at a table on the long veranda and stood as they approached.

Tiana made the introductions, and Professor Revere showed them to seats around the table and fetched a jug of iced juice.

"I take it, Mr Hendrick, that you're here in a professional capacity?" she said as they seated themselves at the table.

"Not at all. I'm a friend of Tiana . . . and I'd like to assist her in locating Lalla Vaugines."

"And now," Professor Revere said, "Lalla's mother too."

"What makes you think that she's—?"

"She never normally leaves her house, Mr Hendrick," Revere interrupted, "other than to attend church. Cristiana is not that old—in her sixties now—but she's suffered health problems of late. She just wouldn't leave like this without telling me." She indicated a neighbouring villa through the trees. "She lives there and I usually see her every day."

"When did you last see her?"

"Two days ago, and she didn't mention going away." She paused. "When I went over yesterday, she didn't answer the door. I was worried, so I went in. I have a pin, you see, for emergencies. The house was empty."

"No signs of anything untoward? No break-in, evidence of a struggle?"

"No, nothing of the kind. But—and I found this odd—Cristiana kept her medicine in a cupboard in the bathroom. She showed me where it was so that, in an emergency, I might administer her daily injection. And the medicine was still there."

"What's wrong with her?"

"She has leukaemia."

"And without her injections?"

Revere looked from Hendrick to Tiana with a worried expression. "She won't last very long at all. She would have taken it with her had she gone on a planned trip, you see."

"Have you contacted the local police?"

"Of course, and they said they could do nothing until she'd been missing for a week. They told me not to worry. But I *am* worried. And now Lalla . . . "

Tiana said, "I haven't seen her for three days."

Hendrick said, "What do you know about Cristiana's involvement with the Church?"

"Very little. She and I are close, but she knows my views on religion, and especially the tenets of her church, so she never mentions her beliefs to me." Revere looked at Hendrick, her blue eyes forthright. "Why do you ask?"

"I'm just trying to put the pieces together. Cristiana was involved with the Church, against the better judgement of her daughter. Lalla vanished, and now her mother. It occurred to me that Cristiana might have tried to locate her. Or perhaps they've simply gone off together."

"Without Cristiana taking her medicine?" Revere sounded dubious.

He drank his juice, a thin, bittersweet liquid that quenched his thirst. "That is disturbing, yes."

Revere was silent for a second or two, her white teeth worrying her bottom lip. At last she said, "There was something . . . I dismissed it at the time. A few weeks ago, I was having lunch with Cristiana over at her place. She seemed distant, not her usual bright, intellectually enquiring self. I asked after her health, thinking she might be in pain. She tends to suffer in silence, you see."

"And?"

"And she told me that she had no worries at all concerning her health, and that soon 'all that will be cleared up'. Which struck me as odd, as Cristiana's leukaemia, though kept in check with drugs, will one day kill her . . . " She lifted a hand, smiling at him to cover her distress.

"Was that all?"

"No. She went on to mention the Avoel and what they believed. Before she retired, Cristiana lectured in comparative cultural studies at the university. She was very knowledgeable about the Avoel and their ways, which I suppose is where Lalla picked up her interest in the aliens. Anyway, she mentioned that the Avoel do not believe in death, which struck me as odd, at the time—coming, as it did, so quickly after what she'd said about her own health."

28

"What do you think she meant?"

Revere hesitated, taking a drink of juice. She stared off into the distance, as if reliving her conversation with the missing woman. "She told me that the Avoel believe in a form of reincarnation, which was news to me, as I understood that the religious beliefs of the aliens are animist."

"A *form* of reincarnation, she said? Did she explain what she meant?"

"No. And I received the distinct impression that Cristiana thought she'd told me too much already."

Tiana glanced at her wrist-com. "We'd better be heading for the station, Matt." She smiled at Revere. "We're taking the train to Allay at two. I think—I *hope*—that we might be able to find Lalla there."

Revere smiled. "I wish you luck, and if there's anything at all I can do . . ."

Hendrick thanked her and they took their leave. They headed for the station via the hotel to collect his case, and caught the two o'clock train to Allay.

FIVE

THE MONORAIL FOLLOWED THE LENGTH of the escarpment for five kilometres, hugging the incline and descending obliquely, and on reaching the plain turned north and gained speed. Hendrick had expected some ramshackle collection of carriages, as might befit a sparsely populated backwater colony world, and he had been surprised to find a sleek white bullet train waiting at the station platform.

Its speed was impressive too; the town of Allay was over seven hundred kilometres north of Appallassy, and the journey would take a little over two and half hours. The carriage was almost empty but for themselves, and they sat at a window table and watched the jungle flash by outside. Occasionally the rail ascended above the canopy, affording spectacular views of the extensive jungle, and then burrowed back into the aqueous, arboreal gloom. Hendrick kept an eye out for any sign of the aliens but saw nothing other than long-legged, red-and-white-striped bovine analogues pasturing beside the track.

Tiana called up a map on the tabletop and indicated the town of Allay. "We'll arrive in the late afternoon, which will give us time to buy provisions and hire a truck."

"You've got it all planned."

She smiled. "I've never been into the jungle this far north before, so it's all new to me. But Lalla told me all about what she does, where she hires vehicles."

She tapped the map north of Allay. "See this triangle next to a tumbled stone symbol? That's the Avoel ruin where Lalla made her base. We'll try there first."

He studied the map. "There's a track that deep into the forest?"

She nodded, her bottom lip trapped between white teeth. "It's not marked but there's an unmade road that passes close to the ruin. The track was used by prospectors in the early days, before they realised there was nothing to prospect."

"Travel would be a damned sight easier if the Avoel didn't proscribe air-cars."

"Makes sense from their point of view, though. Would you want interlopers flying all over your planet?"

He smiled. "Of course not. Especially human interlopers."

He watched the passing jungle, then said, "So, what do you make of what Dr Revere said?"

"I've been thinking about that, Matt. I have an idea . . . See what you think."

"Go on."

"Well, how about Lalla's mother set off into the jungle—not alone, but with members of her church on some crackpot jaunt or other—and Lalla found out and gave chase? That'd explain their disappearances."

"But why do you that think Lalla didn't tell you where she was going?"

"Two possibilities," she murmured. "Either she didn't want to get me involved, for fear of what might happen to me. Or . . . Or she didn't trust me with the knowledge of what she was doing."

He reached out and squeezed her hand. "I'm sure it was the first. She didn't want you to get mixed up with the threats of the Church."

She nodded. "Maybe . . . "

They fell silent. Hendrick watched the gloaming jungle strobe by beyond the window. He closed his eyes, lost in thought. At one point, a train travelling in the opposite direction slammed past, gone in a second and startling him.

Tiana laughed. He looked at her. "What?"

Under the table she slipped off her plimsoll and lodged her foot against his crotch. He stroked her skin. "You were miles away, Matt. What were you thinking about?"

He shrugged. He'd been recollecting, in an involuntary flash, their lovemaking last night—Tiana's almost trancelike absorption in the pleasures of the flesh. It had occurred to him that he hardly understood this small woman, that she was almost as alien to him as the true aliens of this world.

31

He shook his head. "My mind was a complete blank."

She watched him, her head tipped to one side.

"What?" he said at last.

"Last night, back at the hotel, you said you'd tell me what you're doing here. Well?" He hesitated, looking down at her red-painted toenails lodged between the material of his trousers. Her feet were tiny and perfect—miniature representations of the person herself. He could not help contrast this woman with his ex-wife. Maatje was tall, broad, blonde—in her younger days, a member of the Dutch volleyball team, but now just a keen amateur athlete. No, not now. He'd meant five years ago, when she'd left him, repelled by dissatisfaction with the stultifying routine of married life and lured away by someone who promised the intellectual stimulation that he, Hendrick, could not provide.

Tiana prodded his crotch with her bare foot. "Well!"

"Hey, you're a violent woman, Tiana Tandra!"

"Why did you come to Avoeli, Matt? Who are you trying to find?"

"My wife," he said. "Or rather, my ex-wife and the man she was with."

She cocked her head. "Why? To get her back? How romantic . . . or insane."

"No, not to get her back—to get my daughter back."

"Ah . . . " She tipped her head back understanding. "That makes sense. Did they take her illegally?"

"You could say that, yes."

"Tell me about her?"

"My daughter?" The very words opened a pit of pain in his chest. He wished he'd refused to open up to Tiana's enquiries, even if that would have seemed rude. "She's ten and blonde and very pretty and precociously bright, and I miss her like hell."

"And your wife?"

He smiled. "She's thirty-five, tall and blonde, very intelligent, and I don't miss her in the slightest. Not now."

"And the bastard she's with?"

He shrugged. "He's a brilliant man, both a surgeon and an artist." He shrugged. "So how could I compete?"

"I'm sorry," she said in a small voice. "So . . . what are they doing on Avoeli?"

He considered the question, then said, "Running away, Tiana . . . Running away in order to . . . " He stopped.

"What?"

"In order to live," he temporised. There was no way he was going to tell her the real reason they were fleeing from Earth.

That would be just too painful.

"Matt?"

"Yes?"

"I . . . I just want to thank you for doing this, for helping me find Lalla."

He felt a sudden pang of guilt. He soon quashed it and changed the subject. He told her that Avoeli reminded him of a jungle world he'd been posted to in his early twenties, and Tiana listened to him, rapt, for the rest of the journey.

———

Allay was a small town built in the loop of a wide river. Founded on the waterway in the first decade that the planet was settled, the settlement was now a backwater in every sense of the word. It was little more than a glorified village, home to families that had lived there for generations and farmed the surrounding land.

They left the station and strolled towards the riverfront, along which most of the town was situated. The buildings were single-storey, timber, and tumbledown, painted in the red, white, and green of the planetary flag. Motor rickshaws buzzed along the wide streets, and market stalls stood on every corner.

Fomalhaut, a molten dome on the horizon, was setting on a long Avoeli night, though Tiana assured Hendrick that it would be twilight for a good few hours yet. "Just enough time for us to find a hotel for the night and hire a truck for an early start."

"Couldn't we set off now and rest up when it gets dark?" Hendrick asked.

"We could, but that'd mean we'd have to sleep in the truck. And a hotel bedroom would be more comfortable. Anyway, it's only eight hours from here to the temple site. If we set off at dawn, we'll be there before midday."

He glanced behind him, in the direction they had come from the station.

"What?" Tiana said, following his gaze.

"Nothing," he said, not wanting to alarm her.

They set off again, and Tiana led him to the idyllic waterfront and a rooming house built on stilts out over the placid waters of the river. As they approached the green-painted frontage, Hendrick contrived to slow down and glance into the window of a store selling outboard motors. He looked back along the pot-holed road in time to see a distant figure slip behind one of the sentinel palms that lined the street.

Tiana paused in the entrance to the hotel and looked back. "Are you coming, Matt?"

He followed her into the hotel and Tiana spoke in Malagasy to a smiling girl at reception. A minute later they were ushered upstairs to a big, bare double-room looking out over the river.

"Now," Tiana said, "how about we hire a truck then find a restaurant? Lalla said there are some places that do great fish dishes along the river." She looked at him. "Matt?"

He decided there was nothing to be gained by not telling her. "We were followed from the station."

"Are you sure?"

"I know when I'm being followed."

"So, what do we do?"

He'd already thought about that. "I'll leave in five minutes, draw whoever it is away from here, and then try to find what the bastard wants—or rather, who sent him to trail us."

Her eyes were wide. "Be careful, Matt."

"I will," he said. "Once I've gone, give it ten minutes and then go and hire a truck. Only don't come back here. Take our bags and book in somewhere else. Contact me once you're in the new place."

She nodded. "Who do you think . . . ?"

"I don't know. Someone from the Church? I'll have a better idea once I've apprehended him."

He smiled at her shocked expression, crossed the room, and held her. He kissed her forehead and told her not to worry. "I'll see you later, then we'll go out and have a beer or two, okay?"

34

A minute later he slipped from the room, hurried down the rickety staircase and stepped out into the roseate Avoelian twilight.

The street was quiet, with just a dozen or so locals kicking their heels on the corner of the road leading to the station and a gaggle of kids chasing a football. The small man who had followed Hendrick and Tiana from the station was a hundred metres away, leaning against a palm tree and smoking a cigarette.

Hendrick strolled casually in the opposite direction, making sure the man had plenty of time to see him and follow, then he turned right along the main road and affected interest in every shop window. The goods on display charmed him with both their paucity and uselessness. In one window he saw a single paperback book faded and curled by the sun, a child's plastic car minus a front wheel, an out-of-date softscreen and a furled umbrella.

He moved on, came to the end of the row and crossed the street. He stopped again to stare into the window of a barber's shop and glance along the street. Sure enough, the little man was strolling slowly after him.

He continued along the street. Up ahead he made out a defective holographic display advertising a bar.

He came to the door, slipped inside, and ordered a beer. He sat in a booth at the back of the room, positioning himself so that he could see the street. A dozen dedicated drinkers sat at the bar, more intent on their beers than on the off-worlder. He drank a surprisingly good lager and waited for the man to pass the window.

A minute later Hendrick saw him cross the street and take up his default position, learning casually against a palm tree and smoking his cigarette.

He could see the man, but he knew the man would be unable to see him seated so far back in the shadowy bar. His tail must have been confident that once Hendrick had enjoyed his drink he'd leave the bar and continue on his way.

Well, he was in for a surprise.

Hendrick finished the beer, considered having another but decided against it. He was eager to find out why he was being followed. While he was confident the man was not his physical equal, he wanted to be sober when he confronted him.

He slipped from the booth and pushed through a swing door which led along a corridor to the toilets. Further on was a back door, propped open by a bucket and mop. He stepped out into the warm evening and hurried along a narrow alley. He continued for a hundred metres, then turned left and came to the main street. He pressed himself against the crumbling brickwork and peered around the corner. The little man was still angled against the tree trunk, staring across the street at the bar.

As the night cooled, the locals emerged to promenade, and minutes later Hendrick crossed the road in the cover of a posse of teenagers. He passed down a side street, turned left, and hurried down a street parallel with the one on which the man was stationed.

A minute later, he emerged behind the tree where the man stood.

He waited until the street was clear of potential witnesses then strode up behind the man. He grabbed his right wrist and forced it up between his shoulder blades. He felt the cartilage in the man's shoulder creak in protest. To prevent a sudden cry of pain, Hendrick clapped his hand over the man's mouth, dragging him back into the alley, and slammed him into the wall. He transferred his grip to the man's neck and pinned him in position, lifting him off his feet and rendering him immobile.

Hendrick was surprised on two counts: the man was in his fifties, and impeccably attired in a sharp black suit and white silk shirt. Not the obvious candidate to be trailing off-worlders at the behest of the local church.

"Two ways of doing this," Hendrick said. "The hard way or the easy way. The hard way, you say nothing and I hurt you. The easy way, you tell me who you are and why you're following me, and I let you go."

He eased his grip on the man's throat. "This is——!"

"I don't think you heard me, my friend. The hard way is that I hurt you, and you'll eventually speak. Or the easy way—speak and save yourself a lot of pain."

The man just stared at him, rage in his eyes.

Hendrick hurt the man a little, increasing the pressure on his throat but not so much that he passed out or was unable to speak. He released his grip on the man's windpipe and smiled.

"Now, just who the fuck are you?"

"Go . . . to . . . hell!" the man spat.

Hendrick squeezed again and at the same time went through the man's pockets. He found a silk handkerchief, a credit pin, and an ID card. He peered at the shiny rectangle and saw just enough to make his efforts in apprehending the man worthwhile.

In another pocket he came across a miniature alarm pad.

Shit . . .

The bastard must have pressed the pad when Hendrick accosted him, or soon thereafter, because within seconds he heard a vehicle draw up at the mouth of the alleyway. Four armed police jumped out and approached, stun pistols at the ready.

He lowered the man to the ground. "Your lucky day, isn't it?"

The man arranged his collar, smug satisfaction showing in his dark eyes.

An overweight officer eyed Hendrick and spoke in Malagasy.

Hendrick said, "Citizens arrest. He's been following me ever since I arrived in Allay. I'm Captain Matthias Hendrick, Amsterdam Homicide Squad."

The officer eyed the local and said in heavily accented English, "We detected your alarm. Were you following Mr Hendrick?"

The man avoided Hendrick's eye. In cultured English he said, "I was taking an evening stroll, when this . . . " he spat a word in the local tongue and continued, "attacked me."

The officer's glance shuttled between the local and Hendrick, and he said to the former, "You wish to press charges?"

Just what I need, Hendrick thought.

The man made a show of arranging the lapels of his jacket. "On this occasion, no," he said.

The officer spoke in Malagasy, and the man nodded and slipped away. Hendrick watched him hurry down the alley and turn right along the main street.

The officer said, "ID, Mr Hendrick."

He produced his faked ID-pin, and the officer inserted it into his wrist-com. He read the screen, his lips moving.

"So, you *are* an officer with the Dutch police," he said almost incredulously. "Tell me, Mr Hendrick, what are you doing on Avoeli?"

Hendrick gave him the tourist-enjoying-your-beautiful-world line, and the officer bought it.

"And why might an Avoelian citizen wish to follow you, Captain?"

Hendrick smiled. "I'm sure you don't need to be told that, officer. You do have crime in Allay, no?"

The officer passed him his pin. "I suggest you return to your hotel and take care during your remaining time here, Captain."

Hendrick gave a sardonic salute. "I'll certainly do that."

The officer nodded to Hendrick, gestured to his men, and led the way back to the police van.

As the vehicle drove away, Hendrick raised his wrist-com and got through to Tiana.

"Matt!" she sounded relieved. "Where are you? What happened?"

"I'm fine and I know who was following us. Where are you?"

"Just booked us into a great room next to the river." She gave him directions and said, "But who . . . ?"

He gave a brief resume of his encounter with the well-dressed local and described the man's ID card. "And it bore an embossed cross of the Church of the Ultimate Redemption."

"Well done," Tiana laughed. "Listen, there's a great restaurant in the hotel, and the beer's wonderful. Get yourself over here and I'll buy the next round."

He left the alley and took a circuitous route to the waterfront, just in case the little man in the pay of the Church was fool enough to consider following him again.

So much for the reasonable Father Jacobius . . .

As he approached the hotel, the swollen orb of Fomalhaut was going down slowly beyond the distant jungle.

———

He's fast asleep in the moonlight. I've worn him out. The odd thing is, he's so grateful, as if me making love to him is such a big deal. Well, I suppose it is, to him.

I wonder why he's following Maatje?

38

He's a good man, a very good man. When I find Lalla, I'll tell her, of course. I'll suffer her rage, her jealousy. If I said nothing . . . that would only make my guilt all the worse. Better to weather the initial storm of Lalla's jealousy than to suffer the slow corrosion of guilt.

And it looks as if Lalla was right, all along—looks like the Church is mixed up in something odd. That prick following Matt tonight . . .

Wonder what we'll find out tomorrow?

SIX

THEY SET OFF BEFORE FIRST LIGHT, while the town was still asleep, and Tiana drove the half-track truck along a metalled road for a couple of kilometres and then turned off along a rutted track through the overhanging jungle. Last night over dinner Tiana had told him that when the representative of the truck hire company had asked to see her permit, she'd offered him a cash bribe instead. Hendrick hoped they'd be spared the attention of the local police.

They bucketed along at high speed, the windows wound down to admit a cooling breeze. Fomalhaut was beginning its long, slow climb towards another hot day, and already the temperature was in the eighties. Fortunately, the track was mainly in the shade, with just the occasional ruddy flicker of sunlight penetrating the canopy.

Tiana kept up a steady stream of small talk, telling Hendrick about her childhood and her first meeting with Lalla Vaugines. "We were six," she said, "and just starting school. We were friends from the very first day."

Hendrick smiled. "Love at first sight?"

Tiana laughed. "Well, attraction at first sight. There was something special between us."

"Not wanting to appear prurient, when did you realise . . . ?"

"That I was attracted to Lalla? I was thirteen. We were on holiday, fifty kilometres along the escarpment at the Falls. We'd slip away from our families and go swimming in one of the lagoons. One morning, Lalla undressed and swam naked, and I just watched her . . . " She fell silent, gripping the steering wheel and staring ahead. "She was beautiful and I knew then . . . " She flicked a glance at Hendrick. "Lalla knew what she was doing, of course. She told me later that she'd been attracted to me for months. The following day, she suggested I swim naked, and one thing led to another . . . "

"And you've been together ever since?"

"Well . . . not so much together. We've gone through periods of seeing other people. But we always get back together."

He shook his head. She stared at him. "What?"

"No jealousy, recriminations?"

"Not at all, at least on my part."

"Ah . . . But on Lalla's?"

Tiana shrugged, gripping the wheel. "She resents that I find men attractive. It's caused more than a few rows in the past. There was a time when she wanted us to live together, see no one else." She shook her head. "As much as I love Lalla, I couldn't do that."

"Why not? Surely, if you love someone properly—"

"What does that mean, Matt? Define 'love someone properly'. It's ridiculous. We're not meant to love anyone solely and exclusively. Heterosexual society might try to impose that on its citizens as a means of ensuring a stable family environment in which to bring up kids, but for the rest of us . . . "

"You're right, Tiana. But it comes hard as a paid-up member of that heterosexual society."

She glanced at him. "You're a sad man, Matt Hendrick—travelling light years to win back your wife. Why can't you just give in, accept . . . ?"

"I told you, it's my daughter I want back," he said, attempting to keep the irritation from her voice.

She nodded. "And doesn't a small part of you desire to get your wife back too?"

He stared through the windshield at the rough track between the overhanging trees. "You're right, of course. Christ, you're wise beyond your years. And apologies for sounding patronising. Of course in an ideal world I'd like Maatje to come back to me. But I'm afraid that's impossible."

"You wouldn't trust her?"

"It's not that." He tried to articulate his thoughts. "I'm not sure you can love someone without hating them as well. You . . . You've got to understand and accept the whole person, and as no person is perfect, then there is always something to dislike, even hate, in that person. When you come to understand that, and to accept another's faults, and can still bring yourself to feel love—*that's* what I mean by love." He shrugged. "But . . . But there are some things that you just can't tolerate. And . . . while a part of me does want Maatje back, another part wonders how I could accept the person who did what she did to me. I thought I knew her, knew all her faults, and then she takes my daughter away like that." He looked across at Tiana and shrugged. "And how could I want someone back who did such a thing?"

She was silent for a time, before saying, "Matt . . . I've been thinking. When I saw your wife at the station the day she arrived with her lover . . . "

He glanced at her. "What about it?"

"Well, she wasn't with her daughter. It was just her and the guy. They were alone."

He sighed and shook his head. "Samantha was with them."

She looked confused. "No, Matt. I'm telling the truth. They didn't have a child with them."

He looked at her, wanting to tell her the truth but knowing how painful that would be.

Then he recalled her intimacy last night, her gentleness, and said, "That's because Samantha is dead, Tiana."

She stared at him. "Dead?"

He sighed and stared out into the jungle.

Tiana said, "I don't understand."

So he told her how Samantha had fallen victim to a virulent alien pathogen six years ago while he, Maatje, and Samantha had been living on the colony world of Landsdowne, Beta Hydra X. There was no known cure for the disease, so rather than give in and accept their daughter's death, he and Maatje had elected to have her body stored in suspension, in the hope that one day a cure might be found. Technically, she was dead—her bodily functions were quiescent—though if a cure could be found . . .

In the aftermath of the trauma, his relationship with Maatje—always stormy at the best of times—had deteriorated. In her search for someone who might be able to help Samantha, Maatje had met a surgeon called Emanuel Hovarth.

"Is that who . . . ?" Tiana asked.

Hendrick nodded. "They began an affair. She left me and with Hovarth took Samantha's suspension casket and fled."

"But if Hovarth can help—" she began.

"He can't!" Hendrick interrupted. "I know what killed my daughter, and I know that there's no known cure at the moment. I've done research, spent hours trawling the Web, talked to experts in various fields." He gestured. "I want to track Maatje, bring Samantha back to Earth so that I know where she is, so that maybe one day . . . "

She nodded, then asked, "But what are they doing here on Avoeli, Matt?"

He stared ahead through the windscreen. "That's what I'd like to find out."

—

They drove in silence, Hendrick absorbed in his thoughts. At last Tiana said, "So . . . what do you think is happening here with Jacobius? You've had a night to sleep on it. Why did he have us followed?"

She'd asked the same questions over dinner last night, and he'd said he was trying to work it out.

"I'm still no closer. I never was a deductive cop. I was more the hard worker who beavered away at a problem. Slow but sure, unimaginative but reliable."

She grinned. "A little like how you make love."

"Thank you for that, Tiana."

"Sorry. Anyway . . . "

He shook his head. "It's my guess, and a guess is all it is, that the Church has discovered something about the Avoel—something to do with this famadihana ritual that Lalla was onto. They want it kept quiet, for reasons I can't even begin to imagine."

"And Lalla's mother's disappearance?"

"Well, we don't know that they're linked."

"A bit of a coincidence if they're not."

"But coincidences do happen," he said.

"Which leaves us precisely nowhere," she said, grimacing as the truck bumped over a pothole.

"Until we track down Lalla."

They drove on for another hour until Tiana suggested they stop for a break and eat. Hendrick agreed willingly. They'd grabbed a quick breakfast of fruit and juice in their room before setting off, and he was hungry.

Tiana nodded towards the screen set into the dashboard. A satellite map showed a thin line through a field of green. "See that square symbol? It's an abandoned timber mill, about half a kay ahead."

Minutes later the track widened and a clearing appeared to their right. There was not much to be seen of the old mill—just a skeleton of girders overgrown with creepers and vines. Hendrick might have missed it altogether had he not been looking for the structure.

They climbed out and stretched their legs. Tiana stepped into the shade, found a fallen log, and sat down. She opened a rucksack and pulled out a plastic container she'd had the foresight to stock with wraps and fruit. She passed him a bulb of juice and he remained standing, staring into the alien jungle.

"What did the Avoel think about us coming in here and chopping down their trees?"

"They came to an agreement with our founders," she said. "There was a strict quota; only so many hectares could be felled a year." She shrugged. "In the end, when Telemass replaced starship travel, it became more cost-effective to import building material from nearby colony worlds, and the industry collapsed."

"Is there any industry at all on Avoeli?"

"Practically none. The planet exists on tourism."

"Thank the Fates for Telemass," he said.

She looked reflective. "Yes . . . I dread to think how Avoeli might survive without it. No starship line would find it profitable to service the planet."

"You'd be reduced to a hunter-gatherer existence, like the Avoel," he said.

"'Reduced' is a loaded term, Matt. The Avoel do rather well . . . "

"Point taken."

He chewed on a wrap and turned a full three-sixty degrees, taking in crimson trumpet blooms and sprays of purple fern twice as tall as a man. He saw not a single animal, but their proximity was evident in a series of strident whistles and a strange, prolonged bass note.

He turned to Tiana. "What's that low, deep sound?"

"The Avoel call it a shum. It's a bit like a big toad, only bright blue and blind, apparently. They consider it a delicacy."

She was about to say something else but stopped and stared at a point directly behind him.

Hendrick froze. "What?" he whispered.

"Move very slowly, Matt, and turn around."

"What . . . ?" His back prickled and his first instinct was to dive for the cab.

"It's an Avoel," she whispered. "Directly behind you, about ten metres away."

He turned as instructed, and when he was facing away from Tiana he said, "Where? I don't see . . . "

Then he saw it.

He hadn't expected the Avoel in the flesh to appear so reptilian or so etiolated. He was reminded of an elongated albino frog, upright and bipedal, with black staring eyes and a wide mouth. The mouth was open, showing a nasty array of curved needle teeth.

The creature was watching them, half concealed behind a bush, only its upper half showing. A second later it was gone, and Hendrick jumped in surprise at its rapid motion. One second it was there, and the next it had vanished.

He was aware that his heart was thumping. He crossed to Tiana and sat down next to her.

"That was . . . some experience," he said.

"They're so unlike us," she said, "and yet it's what we have in common with the aliens—our bipedalism and analogous facial features—that points up their alienness." She laughed. "Not an original observation. I'm quoting Lalla."

"She's right." He looked around. "I wonder how many others are watching us?"

"According to Lalla, this deep in the jungle a human is under observation all the time by at least six of the Avoel."

He echoed the number. "Amazing . . . And you say they're peaceful?"

"As babies, Matt. There's nothing to fear."

They finished the meal and climbed back into the truck, Hendrick taking the wheel for this leg of the journey. According to the satellite map on the dash, they'd covered over half the distance to the temple complex. Estimated arrival was in a little over four hours.

Despite Tiana's reassurances as to the passivity of the aliens, it felt good to be on the move again.

"Have you thought of what we'll do if Lalla isn't at the temple complex?"

Tiana kicked off her plimsolls and lodged her bare feet on the dashboard. "There's another, smaller complex deeper in the jungle, about another ten kay to the north. We could try there. Only trouble is, it's not navigable by truck."

"Great. How long would it take to hack our way through the undergrowth?"

"According to Lalla, there's a small track," Tiana said. "But it'd still be a bit of a trek."

"Let's just hope she's at the temple."

The sun rose over the jungle, its full, immense orb taking up a quarter of the sky. The temperature increased. Tiana turned up the air conditioning.

At one point she gestured through the side window at something in the forest. "Avoel, Matt. I counted a dozen of them. It appears we have an escort."

———

Hendrick had expected the Avoel temple to be as overgrown as the timber mill—a victim, over the centuries, of nature's inexorable encroachment. He was surprised, when they left the truck on the track and pushed their way through the jungle, to come across a rearing ziggurat in a vast clearing. The temple was clear of creepers and vines, and its ivory-coloured stone was lambent in the bright noon light.

There was no sign of Lalla or her colleagues.

Hendrick glanced around at the enclosing forest, thinking of what Tiana had said about humans being under observation by six Avoel at all times. She moved off towards the ziggurat and he hurried after her.

As they made a slow circuit, he said, "I thought it'd be covered in creepers like the mill back there."

Tiana shook her head. "Lalla and her team cleared it over the years."

"Not the Avoel?"

"The temple is no longer used by the Avoel."

Hendrick paused and craned his neck to take in the full height of the building. "Are they a devolved race? The level of expertise needed to construct something like this suggests a pretty complex society."

"According to Lalla, the Avoel turned their backs on the ways of . . . materialism, let's say. But she says that they've lost none of their cultural morality in doing so. They're still, despite being hunter-gatherers, a civilised people."

He approached the basal stones of the ziggurat and traced the patterns carved into the rock. He made out complex swirls and interlocking spirals, the work of gifted stonemasons. Further along, Tiana pointed out a procession of figures which, despite being obviously Avoelian, put Hendrick in mind of Egyptian carvings.

When they had made a complete circuit of the temple, Hendrick said, "So, no Lalla."

"I was hoping we'd find her truck in the clearing. She often works in the labyrinth of the temple itself, but even if her colleagues had left with the truck, there'd be some evidence of their presence." She looked at him. "I'd call out, but for some reason it doesn't seem quite right to do so."

He peered into a recess in the stones, a narrow passage retreating into shadows. He was about to suggest they return to the truck for a flashlight when Tiana stiffened. "What was that?"

He looked around at the surrounding jungle. "I didn't hear a thing . . . "

"There. I heard it again."

This time Hendrick did make out a sound: the distant drone of an engine.

"Could it be Lalla?"

"I suppose so, but . . . " She sounded doubtful. "Stay here. Don't move."

She left him standing in the shadow of the temple and darted across the clearing to the pathway through the jungle. She vanished into the fronds, and a second later the sound of the engine cut out.

He expected her to emerge smiling along the path with Lalla in tow, but when she did return, seconds later, she was alone and not smiling. She ran across to him and hissed, "The police!"

He moved instinctively towards the entrance to the ziggurat, but she grabbed his hand and pulled him in the other direction. "They'd find us in seconds, Matt."

They ran around the ziggurat and Tiana pulled him into the jungle. They lashed through vines and lolling fronds, pounding through the padded loam. Tiana jinked this way and that before him. Hendrick did his best to follow. He was exhausted when she finally let up. He came to a halt, panting.

"We . . . We could have waited for them," he said. "Explained we're looking for Lalla. We're doing nothing illegal—"

"Our very presence here is illegal, Matt," She interrupted. "I don't want to be arrested and spend a week in jail."

"They know we're here," he pointed out. "They must have seen our truck . . . "

"They don't know it's *ours*, though, do they?"

He stared at her in the half-light. "How thoroughly are they likely to search? Might they give up and head off?"

"In your dreams. My guess is they'll search the area and then stake out the truck, wait for us to get brave and return."

They fell silent and listened. All he could hear was the booming bass of the toad-analogues. "So what's the penalty for illegally entering the jungle?"

Tiana shrugged. "Depends on the magistrate and what the guilty party was intent on doing. I've heard of people being jailed for up to a couple of months."

"All I need," he said under his breath.

"Shhh!" She gripped his forearm and held on, staring at him.

He heard it too: a footfall close by. He saw the uniformed officer through the foliage and turned to run, but a second later they were surrounded by a dozen green-uniformed men and women.

One of their number stepped forward, and Hendrick was surprised to see the overweight officer from the night before. His sweat-soaked face showed no sign of recognition, however, as he said, "Mr Hendrick, Ms Tandra. This way, if you please."

Hendrick looked around at the dozen rifles aimed at them—overkill, he thought, but it did have the effect of deterring any notion of escape. He looked at Tiana and she nodded.

They followed the officer back to the clearing, where another surprise awaited Hendrick. The man he'd apprehended last night, the middle-aged local in the sharp suit, was leaning against the ziggurat smoking his trademark cigarette.

The officer ordered them to halt and addressed Tiana. "Permits?"

Hendrick wondered how so sweet a face could conjure such an expression of distilled hatred.

"Go to hell," she said.

"You realise," the officer said, "that it is an offence to enter the jungle without a current certified permit, and that contravention of the 'rights and access' edict is punishable by imprisonment?"

Despite the attention of the rifles, Hendrick broke from the group and strolled across the clearing towards the suited man. He was aware of a uniformed cop shadowing him.

"I think I understand," Hendrick said when he reached the smiling man. "A joint operation, not unlike what happened last night? Looking back, I see we were both let off rather lightly. Mr . . . ?"

The man removed his cigarette and grinned, showing impeccable dentistry. "You may call me Mr DeVries," he said. "And you should think twice in future about who you accost, Mr Hendrick."

"I'll accost anyone I know is following me, if for no other reason than to find out exactly what they want."

"Not always a wise move," DeVries said.

He stared at the man. "What now?"

DeVries took a last drag on his cigarette then flicked the stub to the ground. "Now you will be returned to Appallassy under police escort and incarcerated until the next Telemass transmission to Earth."

"I don't think you have the wherewithal to repatriate innocent tourists," he began.

"Take it up with a legal representative when you get back to Earth," DeVries said. "And the matter might be dealt with in a year or two."

The attendant cop grunted something, and Hendrick turned and batted the muzzle of the cop's rifle from his lumbar region. "Chrissake . . . I'm coming, okay?"

He returned to where Tiana was being fitted with a wrist-brace. "The bastards are touchy who they allow into their precious forest," he said.

"I wonder what they're hiding."

A cop snapped a brace around his wrists, and another poked him in the ribs with his rifle. "Move it!"

He winked at Tiana. "Whatever it is, they're enjoying the opportunity to wave their weapons about. They remind me of kids in a playground . . . " He recalled making arrests himself and how annoyed and impotent he'd felt at the wisecracks of nonchalant offenders.

They were marched through the jungle and bundled into the back of a waiting police crawler. A cop fastened his wrist-brace to a metal hook protruding from the seat between Hendrick's thighs and then did the same to Tiana.

DeVries sat in the front passenger seat beside the plump officer. The remaining cops piled into a police van and led the way. The crawler started up and bumped along the track.

Tiana whispered, "I heard what the guy said, Matt." She looked at him and smiled. "Been nice knowing you."

"You too, girl," he murmured, "but we haven't reached the Telemass Station yet."

She tugged at her restraints impotently. "Can't see a way of getting out of these. You?"

He examined the wrist-brace and the hook. "Crude but effective. We used neural-incapacitators back on Earth, which were fool-proof, but these work just as well."

"So it's hopeless," she said in a small voice.

"Only if you allow yourself to think so," he said, hoping he didn't sound sanctimonious. "Think positive. Optimism increases your chances of attainting the desired outcome."

"You sound, if you don't mind me saying, like a self-help manual."

He smiled at her then laughed at her lugubrious expression. "I'm just trying to say, stay alert and consider every eventuality."

She was silent for a while. "I'm sorry I couldn't help you find your ex-wife, Matt," she said at last.

He shrugged. "These things happen," he said flippantly.

She glanced at him quickly, then away. "I have something to tell you…" she began.

The officer in the driving seat cried out in sudden alarm, and Hendrick looked up. At that exact second, something hit the windscreen.

He ducked, expecting the glass to shatter, but the missile merely exploded and coated the surface of the screen with a grey, glaucous membrane.

The crawler skidded to a halt.

The driver exclaimed in his own language, opened the door, and jumped out. He stopped suddenly, as if hit by something, then staggered and fell to the ground. DeVries was already opening the door and climbing out, but froze at what he saw. Hendrick made out a quick white figure approaching the car, then DeVries grunted and collapsed, unconscious.

Hendrick saw fleet movement through the side window. Tiana said his name then cried out as the door on her side was yanked open. Hendrick stared past her at the slim figure of an Avoel staring in at them with its big black eyes. He was conscious that the creature did not have to stoop to regard them.

Tiana backed off, her retreat hampered by the wrist-brace moored to the hook in the seat. As she struggled to get away, the alien leaned forward and spat at her. She jerked and cried out in alarm. The creature looked at Hendrick and spat again. Something sharp hit his cheek and he felt a stinging pain.

His face felt numb. Reality seemed to go into a slow dissolve. It was as if he were experiencing everything at a great remove. His sense of hearing diminished, and then his vision. He was aware of someone fumbling with the wrist-brace that bound his hands. He felt small hands on his body, lifting him. He was cocooned in a silent darkness, and he was only distantly aware of being moved from the vehicle. It was as if his body were lagged in a thick insulating layer that delayed the sensation of being carried.

He felt a mounting panic and waited for unconsciousness to claim him.

———

But unconsciousness never came.

At least he was anaesthetised to all pain, and he ascribed this to whatever poison the Avoel had spat on him. He felt as if he were being carried along at great speed, borne feet-first on a padded conveyor belt. He wanted to call out to ensure that Tiana was with him, but he was unable to initiate the procedure. He was paralysed and experienced a surge of overwhelming panic—both at his disability and at being transported into the unknown by an alien race.

He lost all sense of duration. He had no idea whether they had been apprehended minutes ago or hours. Later, he would claim to have enjoyed the physical sensation, if not the mental. The only comparable experience was when he had undergone an operation to remove a bullet from his shoulder, slipping into unconsciousness as the anaesthetic took effect. Then, the glorious lassitude had lasted for seconds only; now it seemed timeless.

Presumably, he was being carried through the jungle by more than one alien creature, but he could not feel the pressure of their hands nor the impact of their feet on the ground. Only vaguely did he wonder where they might be taking him and why, but it was a woolly curiosity superseded by fear.

When the next sensation occurred, it was so sudden and unexpected as to be shocking. The feeling of forward motion ceased abruptly, and he felt nothing. He was very still, existing in a warm, darkened limbo. He wondered if they had arrived at journey's end.

—

Christ . . .

I'm in a hut somewhere. The Avoel took us. Wait till Lalla finds out . . .

Matt's still unconscious, drugged. At least they haven't separated us.

Thing is, I'm not sure what might have been the best: the cops taking us back to Appallassy and deporting Matt, or this—being taken by the aliens. What the hell do they want with us? Why did they save us? The last thing I saw, before I passed out, were the cops lying in the track. The Avoel just left them there and took me and Matt . . .

But why?

SEVEN

HENDRICK WAITED, and yet again it was a period without duration.

He became aware of the faint light and then the sound. The darkness was gradually replaced by a verdant gloaming, as if he were lying at the bottom of an aquarium. He heard the calls of animals and the dull booming bass note that was like the heartbeat of the jungle. Then bodily sensation returned little by little. He felt solid ground beneath his back. He inhaled the odour of loam and vegetation and another, distinct scent—sour and astringent and unlike anything he'd experienced before.

He blinked and stared up at something a metre or so above him. It was like a visual puzzle, the close-up detail of something much larger. He made out an interlacing lattice of brown threads as thick as his fingers. Then something clicked in his head and he knew he was gazing up at the underside of a sloping, woven ceiling. He was lying in some kind of tent-shaped hut.

Only then did he see the Avoel.

The alien was squatting beyond his feet, watching him with its blank black eyes in its expressionless face. When he lifted his head to look at it, the creature moved suddenly, twisted without standing, and slipped out of the hut. Hendrick realised the source of the sour stench; it was the alien's body odour.

He turned his head, relieved to see Tiana lying beside him. She reached out and took his hand.

He kissed her knuckles. "You okay?"

"I feel . . . still a bit odd. As if I'm not really here." She looked at him. "I wonder why they took us?"

"Ah . . . now that's the question." He looked at the triangular flange that was the door of the hut through which the alien had vanished. "I'm going to take a look outside."

He squatted and moved to the entrance, pushed it open, and stared out. "Christ . . . " he exclaimed.

Tiana called, worried, "What is it?"

"I thought, I assumed, we were on the floor of the jungle."

"We're not?"

"Come and have a look."

He moved from the entrance of the hut and sat down, making room for Tiana.

She emerged and sat cross-legged beside him, exclaiming softly, "It's . . . But it's beautiful."

They were sitting on a bracket fungus perhaps a hundred metres long and as many broad. The bracket or shelf was attached to the trunk of a giant tree, and they looked down on a limitless expanse of green jungle canopy. What was so breathtaking, however, was not the rolling plain of the treetops but the boiling hemisphere of Fomalhaut that spanned the horizon with its slow, majestic geysers of fire and loops of ejecta.

He saw other small huts dotted across the shelf and a dozen Avoel sitting in groups of two or three and talking quietly amongst themselves.

Tiana shook her head. "I never realised they lived like this, Matt. I assumed they dwelled on the ground."

They sat in silence, gazing at the fulminating primary. He looked across at the aliens. It was as if they were purposefully ignoring him and Tiana, as if the presence of the humans elicited no curiosity whatsoever. He realised the mistake of assuming that aliens would react to stimuli as would humans. They were *alien*, after all, and they did things differently.

Tiana murmured, "What do you think they want with us?"

He thought about it. "They took us, Tiana. Just *us*. Not DeVries or the police." He shrugged. "That must be significant."

She looked at him. "They *saved* us from them," she said.

"We could look at it that way, yes."

He reached out and stroked the surface of the fungus. It bore a soft knap, like mushroom-coloured velvet.

She said, "But *why*, Matt? That's what I want to know."

He glanced at the sun. Was it his imagination or did its diameter—from one side of the far horizon to the other—appear broader now?

"Tiana . . ." He pointed. "Look."

She squinted at the sun and then at him. "What about it?"

"We arrived at the Avoel temple complex around midday, yes? We were arrested and the Avoel intervened about fifteen minutes later. How long do you think we were drugged?"

She shrugged. "I don't know. An hour or two?"

He nodded. "That's what I thought. A few hours, at most. So . . ." he said, indicating the fiery hemisphere again, "The sun should be going down, shouldn't it?"

She nodded and peered at the sun. "And it isn't?"

"It's rising, Tiana. We must have been drugged for around thirty hours."

He heard movement behind them, beyond the hut, and turned. A dozen Avoel slipped through an elliptical rent in the bole of the tree, moving with a lithe, bobbing motion as they approached where Hendrick and Tiana sat.

They were followed by a taller figure, who squeezed through the slit with difficulty—a small, dark human with a thin face and a severe crew cut.

Tiana gasped. "Lalla!"

She sprang to her feet and rushed over to the woman. They embraced and kissed cheeks, French fashion. As they exchanged greetings, Hendrick found it touching to witness Tiana's relief at being reunited with her lover.

The dozen Avoel approached him and dropped into squatting postures, staring at him in silence with their vast jet-black eyes.

Their attention was unsettling. He smiled at them, uneasy, then glanced back at the women. Tania grasped Lalla by the hand and they crossed the fungus towards him.

"You seem well, Hendrick," the woman said, business-like. "Sometimes the shelth the Avoel use can leave you feeling nauseous."

They sat down before Hendrick and Lalla turned to the aliens. She spoke quickly in what was evidently their own language, and they rose and padded away across the shelf.

"Thank you for saving us," Hendrick said.

"You should thank the Avoel," Lalla said. "I would have been powerless without them."

"But they acted under your instructions?"

The woman had a rather severe face, whose default expression was one of suspicion. Hendrick wondered if she were wary of all men or just him in particular—and, if so, whether that was because of his relationship with Tiana.

"That is so." She stared at him then said, "Did you wonder how the police managed to track you in the jungle?"

"I hadn't given it much thought."

She gave a superior smile. "At some point, the police must have had access to your ID-pin."

In the alley, back at Allay . . . "That's right."

"They loaded it with a signalling virus. All DeVries had to do was follow the signal."

"Who is this DeVries?" he asked.

"The local police chief and a high-up in the Church," Lalla told him. "I searched you while you were unconscious, Hendrick, found your compromised pin and gave it to an Avoel with instructions to head north through the jungle. When DeVries and his goons wake up, they'll be left chasing shadows."

"Resourceful," he said. "But why go to the trouble of rescuing us?"

She hesitated then said, "I would like you to return to Earth."

He smiled. "In that, you share a desire with the police."

"Return to Earth," she went on, staring at him, "with evidence of what the Church of the Ultimate Redemption is doing here."

"And what is that?"

Lalla's entire demeanour appeared hesitant, unsure—wary not only of those around her but of her own reactions. She said, "You'll find that out shortly."

One of the Avoel returned bearing a woven basket containing a variety of fruit. It placed the basket between Hendrick, Lalla, and Tiana, and then retreated.

Lalla said, "You haven't eaten for a while. We have a long trek ahead of us."

She stood and moved to the edge of the bracket shelf, staring out at the rising sun. Tiana smiled at him, took a fruit, and hurried over to Lalla.

Hendrick ate what looked like an apple but was pulpier and tasted much sweeter. He finished it and only then realised how hungry he was. He took another and bolted it down.

What exactly could it be, he wondered, that the Church was up to here on Fomalhaut IV?

And was it possible that Maatje might be implicated . . . ?

He looked across to where Tiana and her lover were engaged in animated conversation. Tiana appeared to be urging Lalla, her body language almost pleading. Hendrick guessed what was going on: Tiana was trying to convince her lover that he, Hendrick, meant nothing to her. He looked away, trying to work out just what he felt about that.

An Avoel emerged from the slit in the bole and called across to Lalla. She turned and replied in its high, fluting tongue.

She crossed to Hendrick, followed by Tiana. "We must be going."

He grabbed another fruit and stood up. "Where?"

She hesitated characteristically then said, "Underground."

———

Lalla! It's so great to see her . . . and she and the aliens are working together—not that she told me that. The first thing she said—typically—was, Who's the prick? Didn't explain what the hell's going on here, why her alien friends rescued us, or what the Church is doing—just, Who's the prick? Jealous to the last.

So I told her he's a detective, a friend working to help me find her. I asked her what was happening, but all she said was, You'll find out.

I said, I love you, Lalla.

She smiled at last, touched my cheek, and said, Love you too, babe.

And oh, the joy.

EIGHT

THEY DROPPED THROUGH THE BOLE of the tree which was hollowed out in the shape of a corkscrew. Much of the passage was smooth, so that they slipped and slid down. In other places, series of steps had been carved for Avoel dimensions, and these were more difficult to negotiate. Lalla led the way with a flashlight, followed by Tiana and Hendrick, and a dozen aliens brought up the rear.

Even here, Tiana was chattering into her wrist-com, keeping up a running commentary. She reminded Hendrick of a kid with a new diary.

Occasionally, they passed slits in the trunk of the tree, which gave onto other fungal platforms situated below the level of the jungle canopy. After descending for perhaps twenty minutes they came to a vertical slash in the bole through which Hendrick made out the shadowy jungle floor.

They continued the descent. Below ground the spiral was constricted, which made sense; they were descending through what he supposed was the tree's tap-root. The flesh pressed in on them and the spiral became even more convoluted. Hendrick, as the largest member of the party, delayed their progress when squeezing around particularly tight twists. He was relieved when Lalla looked up at one point and gave a rare smile. "We're almost there."

A short while later, she disappeared from view, followed by Tiana. Hendrick arrived at the tight slit through which they'd vanished, and Tiana reached back to take his arm and pull him through. The aliens emerged after him, one by one.

He guessed they had travelled as far underground as the tree was tall. They were standing in a long cavern, its walls curving to a ceiling perhaps five metres overhead. All around, dozens of long, slim stalactites hung like iciles: tap-roots of trees similar to the one from which they had just emerged. It was appreciably cooler down here, and illumination was provided not only by Lalla's flashlight. The walls were coated in a film of sulphurous fungus which gave off a low, lambent glow.

Lalla saw Hendrick staring around in wonder.

"It's algae," she said. "The Avoel grow it down here to provide light."

"Ingenious."

"This way," she said and then set off, followed by Tiana. The Avoel remained behind Hendrick as they made their way through the chamber.

The cavern narrowed after a couple of hundred metres so that they were forced to walk single file. The floor sloped; they were descending even further into the bowels of the planet. He wondered how many other humans had passed this way before him.

Perhaps an hour later the passage opened out again into a vast chamber. They were traversing a natural gallery a third of the way up the side of the cavern, and Hendrick looked down on an idyllic scene. A twinkling silver river threaded its way through the cavern, and a thousand tap-roots hung from the high ceiling. Hendrick judged that the cavern, from one side to the other, was in the region of a kilometre wide. He looked ahead but was unable to make out where it narrowed.

He saw movement to his right, down the slope. The Avoel who had been behind him were now descending to the 'valley' bottom. Lalla and Tiana slowed to watch them.

"Where are they going?" he asked.

Lalla glanced at him. "A slight detour to pay their respects."

"To . . . ?" Tiana asked.

"To their ancestors," Lalla said.

Hendrick kept an eye on the aliens as he walked. The Avoel had reached the river now and were wading through the silver water. They climbed the far bank and approached a hanging root. Rather than tapering to a point like the others, this root bulged at its base. One by one, the Avoel reached out, touched the goitrous tumescence with their fingertips, then tapped their foreheads with a peculiar flicking gesture and moved on. They passed a dozen other roots until they came to the next swollen one, where they repeated the ritual of touching the root and then their brows.

"They think their ancestors dwell in the trees?" he asked.

Lalla glanced at him. "Something like that."

Over an hour later, Lalla called a halt. "We'll take a rest here and eat."

She sat down on a flat rock overlooking the sloping cavern. The Avoel were distant, tiny figures, darting from root to swollen root and observing their bizarre ritual.

Lalla opened a rucksack and pulled out more fruit, energy bars, and small bulbs of juice.

They ate in silence for a while until Hendrick asked, "What exactly is the Church doing here?" He paused and, on a hunch, continued, "Trying to convert the natives, right? Trying to wean them from this . . . this form of ancestor worship?"

Lalla chewed an energy bar stoically before replying, "Quite the opposite, Mr Hendrick. The Church is embracing the practice as their own. And that's the reason I'm so worried."

She pulled a camera from her rucksack, and Hendrick thought that she was about to show him what she'd filmed earlier. Instead she strapped the device around her head and adjusted the settings.

Before he could question her, she jumped to her feet and set off. Hendrick looked at Tiana. "What the hell does she mean by that?" he asked.

"I know as much as you do, Matt," she said and hurried after Lalla.

They had been walking for at least three kilometres before the cavern narrowed to a point and they slipped one by one through a gash in the rock, rejoined now by the dozen Avoel. This channel was narrow, and in places Hendrick was forced to turn sideways to squeeze through.

His legs were aching and his back was raw from constant scrapings when they finally emerged from the corridor. Once again they were in a cathedral-like chamber, though whereas the last chamber had been hung with perhaps a hundred tap-roots, this one was dense with thousands of pendant roots—many of them, he saw, terminating in the odd, tumorous swellings.

They were moving along a worn path halfway up the side of the wall, with a long sloping drop to their right. Due to the density of the tap-roots he was unable to assess the dimensions of this cavern. The roots obscured the view—a bizarre mirror image of the forest above their heads.

61

He expected the Avoel to leave them again and go amongst the roots to observe their ritual obeisance. He glanced over his shoulder, but the aliens were still trotting along behind him.

Ahead, Lalla slowed and signalled for him and Tiana to do the same. She switched off her flashlight, turned, and raised a finger to her lips.

The cavern was so silent that Hendrick's heartbeat sounded preternaturally loud in his ears.

Then, faintly, he made out a sound.

A low chant on the threshold of audibility.

Tiana whispered, "What's that?"

"The Disciples," Lalla replied. "The Chosen Few. Father Jacobius's favoured minority—or, rather, those who have paid to be allowed to undergo the process."

Hendrick said, "Would you mind telling me what the hell you're talking about? Allowed to undergo *what*?"

She regarded him for long seconds. "Allowed to be killed by Father Jacobius," she said. "Killed so that they might live again."

———

I've got to be brief.

Lalla's just told us about Jacobius and what he's doing to his people—or rather that he's killing them. And what the hell did she mean by all that 'so that they might live again'? She's not telling us the whole story . . . That's just like Lalla, keeping things to herself.

Something terrible is happening down here. I'm not sure that I want to . . . The fact is that we're in danger. If Jacobius's people find us . . .

I'm scared.

Right. We're on the move again.

NINE

LALLA MOVED DOWN THE SLOPE and Hendrick stumbled after her, numbed by her words. Tiana came alongside him and gripped his hand, the feel of her warm flesh a welcome reassurance. They were striding through the packed root system, weaving between the tapering roots. As they moved away from the wall of the cavern and the sulphurous illumination, the air became murky. He was gripped by a clammy coldness.

The chanting remained on the edge of audibility; it was impossible to judge how far away the Disciples might be. Tiana tugged on his hand and hissed something, pulling him towards one of the swollen roots. "Look, Matt!"

The dozen Avoel approached the root. One by one, they laid fingers on the fibrous tegument, quickly touched their foreheads, and then moved away.

The fabric of the root had been sliced into ribbons and then braided, plaited around something. As they drew closer and their eyes adjusted to the gloom, they made out what was enclosed within the braided root. Hendrick stared at the upright body of an Avoel, crosshatched by the sliced root and covered by a semi-translucent caul. Its eyes were closed, its mouth open to reveal two rows of small, sharp teeth.

Up ahead, Lalla hissed at them to follow her, and they set off again down the sloping bank of the cavern. They passed more and more root-wrapped and mummified Avoel, and each time the attendant aliens stopped to show obeisance to their dead.

They caught up with Lalla and followed as she wound her way through the stalactite root system. Tiana clung to his hand and he heard her breathing rapidly. He felt light-headed and wondered if it were the after-effects of the alien drug still coursing through his system.

The chanting grew louder, though it was still far off. Ahead, dimly, Hendrick made out an orange glow between the pendant roots. It was such a contrast to the prevailing gloom that he knew it was the result of lighted torches. The idea of a torchlight procession seemed primitive yet fitting.

Lalla was slowing down, almost creeping along. She had dropped into a crouch. She veered right, down the sloping bank of the cavern. Below, the flickering illumination grew brighter. An enfilade of roots shielded what might have been going on down there. Their own presence, Hendrick realised, would be concealed from the Disciples.

Lalla stopped and gestured for everyone to do the same. She crouched behind a swollen root and peered around it mass. She pulled back quickly and waved at Hendrick and Tiana to join her.

Hendrick crept forward and squatted beside Lalla, who pointed down the slope.

In the distance, perhaps a hundred metres away, he made out a procession of humans. They were garbed in cerise robes and washed in the light of the flaming torches they held aloft.

At the head of the congregation, leading the way with torch held high, was a tall grey-haired figure Hendrick recognised as Father Jacobius.

They had gathered in a natural amphitheatre, an almost perfectly circular bowl in the rock formation. Lalla explained in a low whisper, "This is the Avoel's most holy place. According to their beliefs, it is the centre of the universe—the very first place created by their gods. Everything else in existence grew out from this point."

Only then did Hendrick notice that three groups of Disciples carried, on their shoulders, biers laden with what he assumed were corpses, swaddled like mummies in brilliant white winding sheets. Jacobius moved from bier to bier, tracing the symbol of the cross on the chest of each corpse.

Hendrick scanned the crowd for any sight of Maatje, without success.

Lalla went on, "Once a month, the Avoel gather here for the ceremony they call *kashanshar*."

She touched the camera mounted on her forehead like a miner's lamp, activating the device, and fell silent.

As they watched, the human celebrants were joined from all sides by the tiny, fleet figures of the aliens, swelling their number and filling the amphitheatre. Hendrick judged that there were in the region of two hundred Avoel down there, and perhaps fifty humans.

At the far end of the amphitheatre, positioned like the altar of a church, stood a frame lashed together from what looked like lengths of timber. A murmur went up from the congregation, and the mass of human and Avoel down below parted to create a central passage. Three groups of four Avoel processed down the aisle, and each group carried what Hendrick realised—after an initial moment of confusion—was a knotted root system encapsulating an Avoel corpse.

The gathered aliens issued a keening sound, which swelled and, aided by the acoustics of the cavern, seemed to come from all sides at once. The ululation rose and fell. Hendrick thought of it as a lament, but he knew that that was wrong; there was a note of joy in the rising, fluting sound . . . which served only to make him wonder anew at what might be taking place down below.

Lalla whispered, "I was with a colleague a year ago, working with the Avoel nearby, gaining their trust, studying their social systems. I became very close to one particular family . . . They told me of this ritual, which is at the very centre of their lives and beliefs. Kashanshar bears a passing a passing resemblance—with one obvious difference—to the ancient Malagasy ritual of famadihana. I vowed to keep it a secret, at least until I'd learned more about it and attempted to assess what effect public knowledge of *kashanshar* might have on Avoel society. But my colleague . . ." She hesitated and then went on, "He was less circumspect and mentioned the practice to a member of the Church of the Ultimate Redemption. Which was how Father Jacobius came to know . . ." She looked from Hendrick to Tiana. "Jacobius made his own study and drew very wrong—but, to him, useful—conclusions, and set in motion the process being played out here today."

She fell silent and stared down at the amphitheatre, and Hendrick also turned his attention to the ceremony.

The Avoel bearing the roots containing their dead now approached the frame at the far end of the amphitheatre. The keening note soared. The bearers knelt and reverently eased the severed root system upright and propped it in the frame.

They backed away and were replaced at the makeshift altar by another Avoel. This one carried a long blade fashioned from stone.

The Avoel approached the root system and methodically cut away the enclosing strands of braided fibre, slowly revealing and releasing the figure within. Perhaps ten minutes later the task was complete and the Avoel corpse stared blindly out at the congregation.

Hendrick looked at Tiana. Her face appeared almost petrified in the half-light as she gazed at the ceremony far below.

Now would occur the ritual that had most in common with the Malagasy practice of Famadihana, he thought; they would take the corpse of their fellow and bear it aloft in celebration of death, of life . . .

Suddenly, the high fluting note that had filled the cavern for so long cut out. The ensuing silence was startling.

Hendrick felt a tension in the air. It was indefinable, almost unbearable, and he had no idea why he felt this sudden sense of imminence. Evidently, Tiana sensed it too. She gripped his hand tightly and hissed, "Matt . . . "

The four Avoel bearers stepped forward, approached the revealed corpse, and reached out . . .

And the corpse moved. It held out a long, thin hand then lifted a leg, stepped forward, and came into the embrace of each of the four Avoel. The thin high wail went up again, and this time Hendrick heard only the joy and celebration of the miracle of resurrection.

His vision misted and he thought he was about to pass out.

The debris of the root system was removed and the second of the severed root systems was placed in the frame and the ritual was resumed.

"Father Jacobius found out," Lalla whispered, "and initiated his own warped and perverted practice, convincing those in his congregation, the weak and the vulnerable and the ill, that he knew the secret of *kashanshar*—that he too could bless them with renewed life."

Hendrick stared into the amphitheatre as the second Avoel corpse stepped from its erstwhile prison and embraced its saviours. The third root system was propped in place, and the Avoel with the blade stepped forward and began cutting away the caul.

"But . . . " he began, finding his words with difficulty, gesturing at the miracle. "But the dead Avoel have come back to life."

He thought of his daughter, dead these past six years and kept in suspended animation until a cure for her disease might be found . . .

He knew that he should not hope for miracles, but he was unable to stop himself.

Lalla said, "The Avoel were never dead, Mr Hendrick. We assumed so at first—that was what my colleague told Jacobius. We mistranslated what the Avoel told us. Later, I learned the truth."

"The truth?"

"The Avoel individuals placed in the root systems down here are what they call *kassallay*. We would call them shaman. They are drugged, enwrapped in the sustaining roots, and remain here for almost four weeks. They believe they're granted visions of the afterlife and great wisdom, contact with their ancestors and through them foresight into the future of their people. Now they will return to their tribes and be revered and guide their people into the future."

He should have known that some things were just too good to be true . . .

Tiana whispered, "It's remarkable, and beautiful."

"And corrupted by Jacobius to his own selfish ends," Lalla finished.

The third resurrected Avoel joined its fellows. Only then did the second part of the ceremony begin—this one involving the humans.

Led by Father Jacobius, the bearers of the corpses moved down the central channel and climbed the slope of the amphitheatre. When they came to a stalactite root, the bearers stopped and lowered their bier. Jacobius stepped towards the root and made the sign of the cross before it, and four Avoel stepped forward and with speed and dexterity slit the root into a hundred strands.

Hendrick leaned forward, watching with appalled fascination as the first human corpse was lifted from the bier and divested of its winding sheet. Naked, it was placed upright amidst the root's strands.

Father Jacobius knelt and the humans behind him raised their voices in soulful prayer. Jacobius stood then lifted his arms to the heavens.

Then the four Avoel got to work, braiding the fibrous strands with care and reverence around the human corpse, plaiting the roots around its emaciated flesh and prominent bones.

Only then did Hendrick realise that Lalla was weeping beside him. Tiana moved to her lover's side and held her, murmuring her name.

"Father Jacobius," Lalla wept, "persuaded his congregation that he could give them renewed life—life after death. He brought them here a month ago and showed them the miracle of what he called the Avoel resurrection." She shook her head. "He is a cynical, evil con man . . ." She turned and stared at Hendrick and Tiana. "He accepts donations of thousands of units from the Chosen and gives them poison and they die a painless death in anticipation of experiencing afterlife . . ." She stared at Hendrick. "Now do you see why you've got to alert the authorities on Earth to what's going on here? The Church has the police and politicians on its side; we need to get the truth to Earth. Then," she said, staring at the four Avoel plaiting the corpse down below. "Then my mother might not have sacrificed her life in vain."

"Lalla!" Tiana said, shocked, taking the small woman in her arms.

Lalla went on, "Not all the Avoel are happy about Jacobius's interference. They are split on the issue, with a faction opposing human intervention in what is a sacred Avoel ritual." She gestured to the dozen Avoel squatting nearby and staring into the amphitheatre. "The rift threatens to tear Avoelian society apart—yet another reason Earth needs to intervene to stop Jacobius and his Church's sacrilege."

Hendrick stared down into the amphitheatre. "Are these the first humans to be . . . sacrificed?"

"The first three corpses underwent the procedure a month ago," Lalla said, adding bitterly, "And in a few minutes, they'll be . . . unwrapped, and then Jacobius's evil will be revealed to his congregation."

Hendrick stared at the congregated faithful down below, and what he saw made his blood run cold. He had assumed that they had been hidden by the mass of other humans, but as the crowd surged forward to witness the plaiting of the first human corpse, Hendrick made out the tall figure of his wife, Maatje, and at her feet the silver torpedo-shaped suspension pod containing his daughter.

Beside him, Tiana said, "What is it, Matt?"

68

He pointed. "Maatje," he said. "She has the pod, my daughter . . . "

She said something but he failed to make out her words. Fear pulsed through him, then panic. If they were to give Samantha to the alien roots, remove her from suspension for just a few minutes . . .

He had to stop them.

A split second after that thought, another occurred to him: Maatje and Samantha were down there, but where was Emanuel Hovarth?

The answer came a second later, as he turned to Lalla, intending to plead with her to help him stop what was about to take place down there.

"Don't move! Raise your arms and remain very, very still."

Hovarth stood beside a tumorous root, a tall shadowy figure in the half-light of the cavern. Hendrick felt his heart pound in his chest and a rising tide of hatred towards the man who had stolen his wife and daughter.

Hovarth stepped forward, a pulse gun gripped in his left hand.

Lalla made a move. She leapt forward, directing her flashlight towards Hovarth and charging. Tiana cried out in panic and Hovarth fired. An electric crackle filled the air and Lalla collapsed as if pole-axed. Hovarth turned the weapon towards Tiana and fired again, and she crumpled to the ground. Hendrick dropped to his knees before the tiny woman and reached out. "Tiana!"

He felt for her pulse.

Hovarth said, "Stunned, Matt. You don't think for a minute that I'd kill them?"

Hendrick looked around for the Avoel who had accompanied them this far, but the aliens had dissolved into the shadows.

He gripped Tiana's warm hand and stared up at Hovarth. "You can't go through with this!"

"Desperate situations call for desperate measures, Matt."

"You're a surgeon, for Christ's sake. A scientist! You can't believe in such superstition!"

"It works for the Avoel," Hovarth said. "According to Jacobius . . . "

"Jacobius is a liar, a charlatan," Hendrick spat. "If you take Samantha from suspension and subject her to . . . to this farce, you'll kill her!"

Hovarth shook her head. "I'm not a complete fool, Matt. I want proof first."

"Proof?"

Hovarth gestured down the slope with the pulse gun. "Before we consent to have Samantha embraided, I told Jacobius that we want to witness the resurrection of the humans who underwent *kashanshar* a month ago. Then we'll see if there is indeed hope for Samantha"

"You're a fool, Hovarth!"

The man tipped his handsome head, regarding Hendrick quizzically. "I would have thought, with the life of your daughter at stake, you might at least have suspended some of your cynicism and kept an open mind."

Hendrick shook his head. "As much as I'd like to believe, Hovarth—and Christ knows how I want Samantha to live again—I can't accede to this superstitious charade."

"Well, let's see who is right, shall we? Turn around slowly and walk towards the gathering. I can't say that Maatje will be pleased to see you, but it's only fair that you should have the chance to witness your daughter's salvation."

Hendrick remained facing the man. "You can't honestly tell me that you believe . . . ?"

Was that a flicker of doubt that crossed the surgeon's craggy features?

"I'm doing this for the woman I love, Matt," said Hovarth. "You don't know how she's suffered these past five years."

"And you don't think *I've* suffered, you bastard?"

"Turn around, Matt," Hovarth said with what sounded like compassion, "and perhaps you'll witness a healing miracle."

Hendrick's first impulse was to dive at the man, wrest the weapon from his grip, and somehow effect the rescue of Samantha from Maatje and the congregation. His second, more reasoned thought was to obey the surgeon's command, bide his time until the opportunity arose to do something.

He turned to face the gathering down below then began walking.

He calmed his rage as he approached the congregation, and it came to him that it would be rash to act in haste. There was no need to attempt Samantha's rescue—at least not immediately. When the human corpse that had undergone *kashanshar* a month ago was revealed to be well and truly dead, then would be the time to act. In the confusion and rage that would reign then, as the congregation learned of Jacobius's duplicity, he would take advantage of the resulting mayhem and attempt to part Hovarth from his weapon.

Behind him, the surgeon said, "Okay, you can lower your hands now. But remember, one wrong move . . . "

They came to the amphitheatre and the gathering of aliens and humans. Hendrick made out Malagasy citizens and Europeans, towering over their Avoelian hosts. They were so intent on the ritual taking place before them that they hardly noticed his arrival. Ahead, Father Jacobius was chanting something as the four Avoel braided the root strands around the stiffened corpse of Lalla's mother.

Hendrick felt pressure at the base of his spine, and Hovarth whispered in his ear, "Move. Over there."

The surgeon shepherded Hendrick towards the tall figure of his wife, standing at the rear of the gathering. At her feet was the suspension pod, and it was all Hendrick could do to stop himself falling to his knees and embracing the streamlined container.

Maatje turned from the ritual and watched him approach. He had expected a show of contempt, an expression of hatred or disgust on her broad, handsome features. He was surprised when she smiled like some religious convert in the throes of ecstasy. Her face, even in the half-light, appeared radiant, flushed with joy.

"Matt," she said. "This is a miracle . . . "

"It's a sham," he began.

"How can you say that? Cynical to the last. Don't you have any emotion in that cold heart of yours? Any compassion . . . ? How hellish it must be to be you!"

He shook his head. He'd heard these words, in varying combinations, many times before. She had scorned his rationalism, used it against him to distance herself from him after the death of their daughter.

She said, "How did you find us?"

He looked away from her smiling face and focussed on Jacobius, who was uttering rapturous prayer as the aliens completed their braiding of the corpse.

"It's what I did, remember? Find missing persons . . . "

71

He felt a bitter stab of recollection. She had once commented that while his profession was that of finding missing people, he had never succeeded in finding himself.

He went on. "I had a tip-off. I should have known you'd be drawn to such . . ." He stopped himself and then said, "You don't seem that surprised to see me."

She laughed. "Oh, I knew you were on your way . . ." The way she said this, with such certainty, made him curious. He was about to question her when the crowd before him moved as one, led by Father Jacobius. They walked up the incline, up the far bank of the amphitheatre, and Maatje, Hendrick, and Hovarth followed, the surgeon pulling the suspension pod like a sledge.

A minute later they arrived at a bulbous root, and the crowd came to a halt with a collective, expectant murmur. Hendrick was near the front of the congregation now, with a clear view of Father Jacobius and the Avoel bearing the stone blade.

He saw Maatje reach out and grasp her lover's hand. Hovarth's attention was on Jacobius and the swollen root. Hendrick could move swiftly, relieve the surgeon of the weapon, but to what end? In minutes, the truth of the holy man's deception would be revealed to all.

The alien approached the bulging root, blade drawn. Hendrick made out the shape of a human being within the caul, a dark figure crosshatched by the braided root system. The crowd drew a collective indrawn breath as the alien began, with swift slashing moves, to cut the membrane.

Maatje stepped forward, her gaze intent.

Hendrick experienced a swift pang of sympathy for the woman, but it was soon quashed. He knew it was unworthy of him, but he couldn't help feeling that she deserved the disappointment about to be visited on her.

Father Jacobius intoned, "And the faithful will witness a miracle, the resurrection of those death would wish to subdue. Faith is great!" he sang.

Despite what Lalla had said about the pastor being an evil, cynical con man, Hendrick knew that he really did believe that the dead would return to life. The passion of the righteous suffused Jacobius's features as he stared at the working aliens, and his ringing tones swelled in the vastness of the cavern. "And lo! Faith is rewarded. The dead do walk again. Our prayers are answered and our loved ones returned to our loving embrace . . . "

Hendrick stared as the alien, with increasing care, drew its blade closer to the corpse within the root system and cut away the last of the braided matter. His heartbeat was loud in his ears and he felt suddenly dizzy.

He made out the dim human shape, its outline coated in some thin grey covering like a soiled winding sheet. The alien reached out and sliced away this last membrane, and the old man moved his head.

Hendrick gasped, his vision swimming. He felt a surge of disbelief, and a concomitant fountaining of hope. If indeed the dead could be brought to life, then Samantha . . .

Hendrick stared and the head moved again, fell forward—not with life but with the natural momentum of something inert being released from its support. The last of the membrane was drawn from the old man, and the Avoel stood back to reveal a skeletal corpse, its skin decomposing. Then the stench of decomposition reached the congregation, and a cry of mixed despair and rage was heard from a hundred throats.

Hendrick experienced a complex set of emotions as the crowd surged around him: self-loathing that he had submitted to credulity and wish-fulfilment, followed by a surge of hope. Maybe now . . .

He turned to where Hovarth had been standing, intent on surprising the surgeon, knocking him to the ground and grabbing the weapon. In the surging melee, Hovarth, Maatje, and the canister were lost to sight. He heard Jacobius crying, "Have faith! We must not be downcast that this time . . . " But the rest of his pleas were lost in the cries of the enraged congregation.

Then Hendrick caught sight of Maatje and Hovarth fleeing up the opposite incline, hauling the container in their wake. He set off after them, hoping to reach Hovarth without being seen. When he was a matter of metres from the surgeon, however, Hovarth heard him approaching and turned. Hendrick dived at Hovarth, and Maatje screamed at him with despair and anger.

Before Hendrick could stop him, the surgeon raised the pulse gun and fired.

Hendrick desperately reached out for the silver container as the pulse slammed into his chest. He felt himself collapse and slip into instant oblivion.

—

I'm feeling terrible, but at least we found Matt . . . It's chaos down here, but at least it's allowing us to get away without being noticed.

I've got to tell him. I will! Once we get out of here and reach Lalla's truck, I'll tell him what I did, tell him about Maatje, and just hope he can find it in that good heart of his not to hate met.

And then, once Matt leaves Avoeli for Earth, then I'll say to Lalla, No one else. Just you. Me and you. Forever.

TEN

HENDRICK FOUND HIMSELF BORNE ALONG again, carried by more than one person, only this time his senses were not anaesthetised. He felt pain in his chest, where the pulse had impacted, and nausea from the electrical charge that had scrambled his senses. He tried to open his eyes, but the effort was beyond him. At least this time he knew Tiana was with him; he heard her breathing at her side, felt her hand clutching his.

As the pain in his chest mounted, he passed out again.

When he came to his senses, he was no longer being carried. He was sitting upright and being shaken back and forth. This time he was able to open his eyes, and he found that he was in the passenger seat of a truck bouncing along a track through the jungle.

He turned his head. Tiana was driving, staring fixedly ahead. She turned and gave a big smile when he said her name.

"Don't worry, Matt. We got you out of there . . . "

"What happened?" he croaked.

She passed him a canister of water and he drank gratefully. He gasped and took another drink.

Tiana said, "How are you feeling?"

"Rough. Nauseous." He looked at her. The last time he'd seen Tiana she was lying on the ground, the victim of Hovarth's pulse gun. "You?"

"I'm okay. Still a bit scrambled. But it's passing. You'll be okay in an hour or two."

He asked again, "What happened?"

"When I came to my senses, it was hellish down there. The Disciples were fighting among themselves. And Father Jacobius . . . "

"What happened to him?"

75

She shook her head. "He's dead. Someone knifed him." She patted something on the seat beside her. "Lalla gave me the film. She thought it best that you take it to Earth, inform the authorities. Jacobius might be dead and the Church in chaos, but Jacobius wasn't alone in the deception. She says that the authorities need to investigate, get to the bottom of the corruption."

He took another long swallow of water. "I'll do that." He looked through the window at the passing jungle. It appeared to be twilight out there; Fomalhaut's ruddy glow showed as a smear above the horizon. He'd lost all track of time.

"How long have I been out? And where are we?"

"You were unconscious for more than ten hours, Matt. You were hit with a bigger jolt than me and Lalla."

"I was closer," he said.

"We're a couple of hours from Appallassy," Tiana went on. "We've been travelling through the night."

He sat up, recalling his last memory of events beneath the jungle. Hovarth and Maatje escaping with the pod containing Samantha. He felt a surge of despair.

"Maatja, Hovarth . . . ?" he said.

Beside him, Tiana gripped the wheel and stared fixedly ahead. "They got away, Matt. I suspected they left the planet, so I contacted a colleague at the station. They left on the last transmission. He said they were bound for Kallithea."

He tipped back his head and swore.

"But it's okay, Matt."

He stared at her. "Okay? They've got away, fled to Kallithea. When's the next transmission to that godforsaken hole?"

"Not for another week. But you see, it wasn't a direct transmission from here."

He looked at her. Had the pulse charge scrambled his head? "I don't understand . . . "

"They took a cheap transmission to Kallithea via Brimscombe, where there's a day's wait until the onward journey to Kallithea."

"So . . . "

"So if we get you to the station by noon today, you can take the direct transmission to Earth and pick up the Kallithea shot tomorrow. You'll get there just after them, Matt."

He laughed out loud with relief. Despite the ache in his sternum, he was feeling better already.

"Thanks for getting me out of there," he said.

She shook her head. "I couldn't leave you, Matt. And . . . " She stopped.

"What?"

She shook her head, her lips compressed. He saw that she was weeping.

"Tiana, what is it?"

She braked the truck suddenly and sat very still in the ensuing silence, staring through the windscreen and silently crying.

He reached out and touched her arm. "Tiana? What is it?"

"I'm sorry, Matt."

He shrugged uneasy. "Sorry? I don't understand . . . "

She hung her head and murmured, "You'll never forgive me."

"Tell me."

She turned and looked at him, tears rolling down her cheeks. "Last week, after the transmission from Earth . . . A tall blonde woman needed medical assistance . . . We got talking." She shrugged. "We met for a drink later. She told me that someone was trying to find her, a vicious ex-lover. She was running away. She asked for my help. She gave me your description, asked me to contact her if you showed up and followed her."

He nodded. That sounded like Maatje—lying and scheming and using people in order to keep one step ahead of him.

"And when I arrived . . . ?" he asked.

"When I got off shift after treating you, I contacted her, told her you were on Avoeli. She asked me to contact her if you took the train to Allay."

He said, "And you did?"

Mutely, she nodded. "That night, before we . . . before we made love, I told her you'd be aboard the two o'clock train. Matt, I'm sorry! I . . . I didn't know you then . . . didn't know what a . . . a good man you were."

He said, "You weren't to know, Tiana. Hell, I know how persuasive Maatje can be."

"You must hate me," she said almost inaudibly.

"No. No, of course I don't."

She stared at him through her tears. "Honest, Matt? Honest, you don't?"

He reached out and cupped her head. "Honestly, Tiana."

She started the engine and they drove on in silence. Fomalhaut was rising imperceptibly over the far horizon. It would be a sight Hendrick would remember for the rest of his life, an image loaded with a freight of complex emotions.

At last Tiana said, "That night, when I picked you up at the bar . . . "

He glanced at her. "I thought it was too good to be true."

"I was drunk," she said. "I saw you sitting alone. I recalled what Maatje had told me, and somehow her description didn't match the lonely person I saw. I was intrigued, so I introduced myself." She shrugged. "And that night, in bed." She gripped the wheel and went on. "You get to know someone when you're so intimate, and I knew that you weren't the person Maatje had described."

He refrained from asking her what his ex-wife had said; he could imagine the picture she had drawn.

He said softly, "You could have told me sooner, Tiana, that you'd contacted Maatje."

She compressed her lips, avoiding his eyes. "I'm sorry. It's just . . . "

"By that time," he said, "I was helping you, right, and you thought I'd leave if you admitted contacting Maatje?"

She shrugged, swallowed. "No. Maybe. I don't know . . . By that time, I felt something for you. I liked you for the good person you are. And I couldn't bring myself to . . . to have you hate me. I'm sorry. I feel so guilty."

He laid a hand on her leg. "Hey, you're not the only one, okay? I feel guilty too."

She sniffed and looked at him with tear-filled eyes. "You do?"

"When I agreed to help you . . . it wasn't out of altruism, okay? I knew—or rather, I suspected or hoped—that Maatje might have . . . " He shrugged. "I knew she'd come to Avoeli and got herself involved in some kind of alien cult. So, you could say that I was using you too. But, at the same time, Tiana, I honestly wanted to help you, okay?"

She smiled at him. "None of us are perfect, are we, Matt?"

"None of us," he said.

A silence came between them and then Tiana smiled through her tears. "I'd like to keep in contact, Matt, when all this is over. I know you might not want to . . . "

He smiled. "One day I'd like to come back."

She nodded and smiled and backhanded tears from her cheeks.

They drove on, and on the far horizon the giant hemisphere of Fomalhaut rose on another new day.

—

Hendrick stood with the other travellers in the departure lounge of the Telemass Station, as anxious as ever before the imminent translation.

A small figure made its way through the crowd, smiling. Tiana stood before him. She reached out, took his hand, and said, "Good luck, Matt."

He kissed her. "I'll be in touch."

An announcement boomed through the lounge: "Will all passengers make their way to the translation pad. Repeat, will all . . . "

"Say goodbye to Lalla for me."

"I'll do that, Matt."

"I hope you two sort things out."

They embraced for one last time, and Hendrick made his way from the lounge.

Minutes later he took his place among the other travellers on the translation pad, a pre-emptive nausea rising in his chest. He looked up at the window of the observation lounge and made out Tiana's small face. She was smiling down at him sadly. She raised a hand and waved.

The countdown began. "Ten . . . nine . . . eight . . . "

Hendrick smiled, raised a hand and waved at her.

"Three . . . two . . . "

He looked ahead, wondering what might be awaiting him eventually when he arrived on Kallithea.

A second later, he was blinded by the white light.

One second he was standing on the translation pad of the Telemass Station on Avoeli, Fomalhaut IV, and the next he was twenty-five light years away on Earth.

ERIC BROWN began writing when he was fifteen while living in Australia and sold his first short story to Interzone in 1986. He has won the British Science Fiction Award twice for his short stories, has published over fifty books, and his work has been translated into sixteen languages. His latest books include the SF novel *Jani and the Greater Game*, the collection *Strange Visitors*, and the crime novel *Murder at the Chase*. He writes a regular science fiction review column for the *Guardian* newspaper and lives near Dunbar, East Lothian. His website can be found at: **www.ericbrown.co.uk**.